After The Days of Infamy

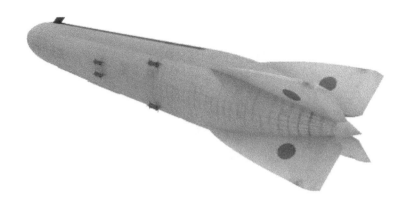

By

A.G. Kimbrough

After The Days Of Infamy

Technical Adviser: Daniel Blumentritt

Cover Graphics: Vasily Tolstikov

Table of Contents

Prologue

December 7, 1941

Captain Minoru Genda smiled as the last plane landed on the Kaga. Both attacks had succeeded beyond his wildest expectations, and the second wave, had not lost a single plane. The losses on the initial attack were much less than projected.

As the four carriers started turning, he saw the smoke rising over the burning ships and oil storage tanks. Even from 50 miles away, and at an 8,000 foot altitude, he could see that the smoke column height was way above his vantage point on the carrier bridge.

After a stop a 1000 miles West of Portland Oregon for their support ships, to resupply fuel, armaments, and replacement planes, the carrier airship fleet will bring destruction to the American West Coast before the end of the week.

1926

Restrictions on German airship construction are relaxed by the Locarno Treaties.

1927

The Helium Control Act, passed by the United States Congress, prohibited the sale of Helium to any foreign government.

1928

The new dirigible, christened Graf Zeppelin in honor of the Count, flew for the first time.

June 29, 1929

The young man slowly became aware of the pounding at the bedroom door. Rionitsi (Rio) Watanobe opened his eyes, looked at the door, and groaned. His best friend, Mitsumi (Mickey) Imazumi, shouted, "Rio, you have a telegram from home. It looks important."

Rio rolled out of bed, leaving the sleeping, naked, blond, who was curled up beside him. He stumbled over to the door, and asked, "What time is it?"

Mickey replied, "It's after 9:00, You need to get going."

He handed the telegram through the partially opened door and noticed the blond.

He said, "You sure don't have time for more whoopee this morning. We have to be at the graduation ceremony no later than 1:00. There's a pot of coffee and sweet rolls in the kitchen."

Rio closed the door and looked over to the sleeping blond.

"Wake up Betty, get dressed and go downstairs to get me some coffee and a roll. I need to read this."

She opened her eyes, stretched, and replied, "Don't you want a little more loving?"

Rio thought she looked like a big, dangerous feline. After admiring the view for a few seconds, he said, "Sorry honey, but I have too much to get done this morning."

Rio walked over to his desk, opened the thick envelope, and started reading. The telegram was from his father, the owner of the largest coal mine in Japan, and the Director of the Japanese Government's Critical Resources Ministry.

The telegram directed him to cancel his return home after receiving his Geology degree. Instead, it directed Rio to travel to Texas, and secure the services of a modern mobile exploratory oil drilling rig, and an experienced operator.

The telegram stated that the government will pay up to double the US rates and cover all transportation and operation expenses. The drilling rig would be used to expand Japan's petrochemical resources. Japan will supply all support labor as well as the production drilling rigs.

Rio frowned, and realized that his plans to return home on a luxury passenger ship, with a stop in Hawaii, were going to be canceled.

When Betty returned with the coffee and a sweet roll, Rio kissed her, and gave her a fifty-dollar bill for the cab fare, and said goodbye.

Betty Lawrence was one of many aspiring starlets, who

were struggling to be discovered. Rio had dated her over the last two years and thought she was not a typical dumb blond. She had a quick wit, and native intelligence that he appreciated. They were friends, in addition to being compatible lovers.

After a shower and dressing, Rio came downstairs, and found both Mickey and his other roommate, Heinrich Lehman, eating breakfast.

Rio and Mickey had been friends since they were six, when they both attended an exclusive school designed to develop Japan's future leaders. They had shared a large rented home in Beverly Hills with Heinrich Lehman, since they arrived at UCLA for their last two years of college. As part of a handful of foreign students they naturally gravitated to each other.

Mickey is the son of the largest Mitsubishi stockholder and Heinrich is the son of a large Zeppelin stockholder.

All three wealthy young men enjoyed living in Southern California during the Roaring 20s.

Rio told Mickey he would not be leaving on the ship with him and asked him to look after his trunk. Rio would take only a suitcase on the train to Texas. It turned out Heinrich would be on the same train until they reached Denver, Colorado. At that point Rio would change to a train headed South to Texas.

In a final party after the Graduation Ceremony, they enjoyed the company of their girlfriends, who knew there were no string attached to their temporary relationships with these wealthy young men.

The next morning Heinrich and Rio joined Mickey in a cab ride down to Long Beach and dropped him off at his ship. After a lunch in the harbor, they made it to Union

Station with 15 minutes to spare.

The train ride was long and might have been boring except for a high stakes poker game in the club car. The next morning Rio watched the country roll by while Heinrich attempted to develop a relationship with a young woman who would be riding to New York with him on the same train.

Rio knew how big the United States was, but to experience the vastness of the mountains and the high plains, astounded him.

He was exhausted by the time he reached Dallas Texas and spent a full day resting in his hotel room. He did spend time looking through the Dallas Yellow pages searching for Drilling Contractors.

July 2, 1929

When Wade Callahan returned to the rig builder's office, there was an urgent message waiting for him. There had been an explosion that morning at the drilling rig, and his father was killed. The drive from Houston to the drilling site took six hours, and the sun had already set when he arrived.

During the long drive Wade reflected on the man he loved and now had lost. His Mom died in the 1918 flu epidemic when he was 12, and, except for school, he was always with his father, a moderately successful Drilling Contractor.

Ralph Callahan had been a successful wildcatter until he went bust on the fourth successive dry hole. It took him two years to earn enough to buy his own drilling rig, which he operated by hiring it out to other wildcatters. That arrangement got him paid even if it was a dry hole. If the well came in, the bonus was gravy.

Wade was running a shift on the rig by the time he was 16 and was now a full partner in his father's company. The new drilling rig was planned to allow him to double the companies cash flow by drilling two wells at the same time.

The next morning, Wade drove out to the rig, after checking on the lone survivor who told him they hit a high pressure gas pocket, and the blow-out preventer failed. The explosion was triggered 30 seconds later.

The rig and most of the equipment would be a total loss.

Wade buried his father next to his Mother two days later.

The owner of the mineral rights at the well site, walked away and disappeared, without making a final payment. The insurance on the rig, and his father's life, barely covered the immediate expenses.

There was no way Wade could continue the progress payments for the new rig, and he planned to sell the few remaining assets and look for a job. The trailer his dad used for an on-site office had been blown over by the blast, and Wade spent a morning getting it back on its wheels. He was going to live in the trailer for a few days before holding an auction of the remaining assets.

When Wade turned the cot back over, he noticed the safe his father used to hold the weekly cash payroll. He used the key from his father's key-ring and opened the safe. Inside, he found $565 in cash and a large envelope containing several stock certificates. Their value had skyrocketed along with rest of the market over the last three years. The sale of the stock produced enough cash to pay for the new rig and have a little left over for operating funds.

After The Days Of Infamy

July 6, 1929

When Rio arrived in Houston, he realized five weeks of running newspaper ads, had proven unsuccessful, in finding a driller willing to go to Japan, even at double Texas drilling rates.

August 8, 1929

Mickey received a telegram from Heinrich at his Mitsubishi Tokyo office. The telegram said that Heinrich will be a crew-member on the Graf Zeppelin airship when she visited Tokyo. Heinrich offered to give Mickey a guided tour of the airship while he is there.

August 18, 1929

Graf Zeppelin arrived in Tokyo, and Mickey spends most of the next day in a detailed tour, of the airship, conducted by Heinrich. Mickey is amazed at the precautions to prevent a fire on the airship. Before he could leave the passenger area of the gondola, he had to change into a set of coveralls, which contain no metal at all. He also has to wear a pair of felt slippers instead of his shoes.

The airship's internal construction fascinates Mickey. He learned that the five Maybach engines could be fueled by both gasoline and propane. The propane is stored in several internal gas bags, and since it weighs almost the same as air, as it is burned off, it doesn't change the airship lift. That action does not require exhausting the hydrogen lift gas, to avoid increasing the airship's altitude.

During the airships stay, Heinrich stays with Mickey in his penthouse, and is given a guided tour of the city and the Mitsubishi aircraft production facilities. The men's friendship deepens, and they promise to stay in contact.

A.G. Kimbrough

Heinrich promised to give Mickey a tour of the Zeppelin works any time he comes to Europe.

August 19, 1929

The new rig is almost ready to be put to work, but Wade has been unable to find an exploration project for it. Texas currently has an oil glut, and no one wants to spend money on exploration wells while the oil price is so low, and the Stock Market is soaring.

August 21, 1929

Wade receives a call from an old friend who used to work for his father.

"I'm sorry about Ralph, he was a good man. Are you still looking to put your new rig to work? I ran across a young guy named Rio Watanobe. He's from Japan, and has been trying to hire an exploratory driller and rig to look for new oil deposits, in Japan. He said they are willing to pay double the current Texas rates. If you're interested, he's going to be at the Hilton here in Houston for a couple more days."

Rio was discouraged by his failure to achieve his father's objective. The prospect of a minimum five year commitment had discouraged the few Drilling Contractors who responded to his adds. Even the offer of a substantial bonus at the end of the contract failed to make a difference.

He was starting to plan for his return in failure when the phone range in his hotel room.

Two hours later, he met Wade Callahan to discuss the opportunity. It took all afternoon to hammer out the details, and both men agreed to meet at Barclays Bank the next morning, to transfer the initial payment, and sign the final agreement.

Rio was elated at the success of his mission and sent a telegram to his father reporting it.

The next morning, a telegram from his father directed him to contact the Japanese freighter, Honshue Maru, and book passage for himself and Mr. Callahan. The ship was waiting in New Orleans, and was scheduled to carry the rig and all its equipment, including 5000 feet of drill pipe.

Later that day, with the funds transferred, and the agreement signed, the young men enjoyed a Texas steak dinner together. While it wasn't Kobe Beef, Rio enjoyed the dinner, and the company of his new American friend.

August 30, 1929

After a frantic effort to get everything to New Orleans and loaded, Rio and Wade board the Honshue Maru, bound for Japan. They are the only passengers and share the Captain's cabin. The ship's primary cargo is Wade's new rig and all the necessary support equipment.

October 24, 1929

The US stock market crashes, with world-wide implications.

November 3, 1929

Honshue Maru arrives in Japan. Rio and Wade are the same age and have become good friends during the voyage. Wade has learned to enjoy some Japanese food and started to pick up the language. They part company, promising to stay in touch.

Rio found his father was not in Tokyo and spends a day

with Mickey before returning home. He also receives an award from the government for his work in securing a drilling contractor.

An English speaking representative of the Petroleum Industry takes Wade in tow and assists him in the logistics of getting his rig and support equipment through customs and shipped to the drilling site.

November 5, 1929

Rio had been surprised that his father was not in his Tokyo office. His assistant said he had returned home to deal with some problems at the mine.

His father was waiting in his limousine, at the ferry landing. By the time they reached the family home, Rio understood the gravity of the situation. The world-wide market crash had wiped out 80 percent of his father's fortune, and Japan's economy was in trouble. The primary vein at the mine had gone deep, and soon its coal could not be extracted at a cost that was profitable.

The wealth his father spent 40 years building, was mostly gone, and he was depressed.

Rio went to work immediately to improve the mine's productivity. The mine had suffered over the years that Rio had been away in school, and his father's immersion in the Ministry in Tokyo.

The mine manager was a long-time friend and employee of his father.

An audit commissioned by Rio, revealed that the manager had been embezzling company funds for years.

Rio went to Tokyo, and in a fiery meeting with his father, demanded that the manager be sacked. His father refused to believe the charges and flatly refused to consider firing him. At that point, Rio threw the auditor's report on the desk, told his father he quit, and stormed out of the building.

Rio was staying with Mickey, and the next morning his father called Mickey and asked him to talk Rio into returning.

The following day Rio met with his father again, and they spent the next two days in deep discussions about their future. His father was overloaded with his government duties and depressed about the loss of his families fortune.

He deeply loved his son and was proud that he had stood up to him. By the end of the second day, they signed an agreement transferring total control and ownership of the mining operations to Rio. His father also promised to never interfere in those operations.

Rio returned to the mine, fired the manager, and three of his accomplices. Over the next year, He struggled to return the mine to profitability. The Japanese economy was still in shambles, the price of coal low, and the coal seams were now so deep they were becoming uneconomical to extract.

With his efforts providing diminishing returns, Rio decided to explore alternative, undeveloped mining sites.

November 30, 1929

After too many delays, Wade has the rig and support equipment in place at the first drilling site, and starts drilling operations.

He brought his almost new Ford pickup, which proved invaluable in running errands locally. He also brought an older International flatbed one ton truck, which had an arc welding rig and a big Detroit Diesel generator mounted on its bed. He thought the generator was overkill, but it was paid for, and it would power the drilling rig if they needed to operate in a remote location without power access. When he learned that Japan had only 50 cycle power the generator prevented him from having to replace all the electric motors on the rig.

Because of the limited experience of his locally recruited Japanese crews plus the language barriers, it was necessary for him to be present any time the rig is operating, Wade purchased a small trailer to use as an office and a bunkhouse. Other than occasional progress meetings with his client, his activities outside the drill site were limited. The nearest restaurant delivered his meals, and he rarely went over to the nearest town.

December 1931

Rio's search for a new mine location revealed a promising deposit just outside the hamlet of Takinoue. It was seventy-five miles Southeast of the existing mine and had a good access road. The problem, was the unknown size and depth of the deposit. It took almost a year to survey and determine that the near surface coal was limited to a 2000 foot circle on the side of a ridge. Before he could spend the expense of opening a production mine at that location, he needed to know how deep the seam extended.

Rio spent six months researching ways to make that determination without the major expense of sinking a shaft to the bottom of the seam. His Geology instructor at UCLA sent him an article about using an oil drilling rig to survey the size, depth, and quality of ore deposits.

He hadn't seen Wade Callahan since his arrival in Japan, and he decided to contact him and get his opinion.

Discovery

December 15, 1931

When his client went into bankruptcy, the court canceled Wade's last drilling contract. He blamed himself for not seeing the risks of signing that contract. The last three dry holes confirmed that the countries oil deposits did not extend beyond the field already in production.

His new client was the second to assume his original contract. Although the geology in his lease did not look promising, he had seen successful wells in other unpromising areas. They were only down 500 feet when he received the notice that his contract is in default because his client declared bankruptcy.

That was the point when Wade discovered that the original contract provision to compensate him if the contract is terminated early, would not apply in case of a bankruptcy. The compensation would have been equal to a year's operation plus the costs to transport himself and his rig back to the US. The liability of his first client ended when the second one assumed the contract.

Now, because no other company would assume it, he was stuck, with no one to even pay the costs for shipping his rig and equipment back to the states. All the promising fields were already in production, and the only interest he found was to drill an offshore well. Wade was unwilling to risk his rig attempting to drill from a floating barge, particularly with no one available who had offshore drilling experience.

The industry thinking, was, that there was little chance of locating another on-shore field, and no one was willing to spend more money with this Gaijin from Texas.

Wade was getting desperate, since no other projects were in sight, and without the final bonus, he was not sure he could even afford to ship his rig back to Texas. When he returned to Tokyo to attempt to find a Japanese buyer for his rig and supplies, there was a message for him to contact Rio.

Two days later, Wade visited the potential mine site with Rio, and agreed to accept a drilling contract. While Wade did not believe he might hit petroleum assets, he used his standard Texas contract that called for a 15 percent commission on the value of all petroleum assets recovered from the wells for a period of five years after the well completion date. He could not get his prior Japanese customers to accept that part of the contract, but Rio agreed to it with the added words, "Except for Coal Deposits."

April 28, 1932

Drilling at the new mine site started in the center of the

surface coal deposit.

At 100 feet, the drill bit encountered a small natural gas pocket, and Wade insisted they install a blow-out preventer. The needed preventer was not available, in Japan. He had to order one from Texas, and it added costs and caused a month's delay.

July 15, 1932

The coal vein had continued as the drill bit descended. At 1500 feet, the drilling stopped for the annual Ocean Day traditional holiday weekend in Japan.

Rio returned to the drilling site early in the morning after the holiday. He directed Wade to have the crew use their last 500 feet of drill pipe to finish that part of the evaluation. before drilling two more exploratory wells at the edges of the surface deposits.

The two men are having a last cup of tea when the 4.5 quake hit.

The quake was unusual for the area, but they didn't think it was a big deal, until a high-pitched scream came from the drilling rig. Both men ran out of the field office trailer. They could see a plume of moisture coming out of the well. Wade shouted at Rio to keep everyone away and raced to the well base. He had the flow cut off within a half hour.

Rio ran up to the rig after the gas flow stopped and was surprised to hear Wade speaking in a high squeaking voice.

"We struck Helium! The only other place you can find it in the world is at a field in the Texas Panhandle. It's not good for much except filling kids balloons. Oh, the Germans might be interested in using it instead of Hydrogen to fill their Zeppelins. The Navy won't let them buy any from the

US."

August 20, 1932

It took a month to cap the well and install equipment to compress and transfer raw gas from well to storage bottles. The gas sample tested, to have a twenty-five percent natural gas content, which is removable, but the equipment to do it is not available in Japan.

Rio took the train, a ferry, and another train to Tokyo for a meeting with Mickey. A cable to Heinrich resulted in a request for an immediate shipment of a full shipload of raw gas bottles. The gas should be delivered in Hamburg by Rio and Mickey, with the price negotiated after arrival.

A call from Rio to Wade at the well site directed him to run a 24-hour shift filling gas bottles and shipping them to the Port of Tomakomai. He also directed Wade to drill the second exploration well as soon as he could get more drill pipe delivered.

Rio stayed in Tokyo, arranging for a large freighter, and using both his father's and Mickey's influence to locate all the gas bottles available in Japan, and ship them to the well site.

September 5, 1932

Rio and Mickey, and the ship-load of gas bottles, filled with unprocessed Helium gas, departed the Port of Tomakomai for Homburg Germany.

October 30, 1932

The freighter arrives at Homburg with Rio and Mickey on board. Heinrich is waiting at the dock and takes them to the Zeppelin headquarters.

Over the next six weeks, the discussions include the Zeppelin Board, the Ministry of trade, Karl Dönitz, and Hermann Goring. They signed the final agreement on December 15, 1932.

The Agreement includes, a license to Mitsubishi for manufacturing Hindenburg class airships, and the under development, JU 87 (Stuka) dive bomber, plus a substantial price for each shipload of liquefied, processed gas. In addition, the agreement also forbids any disclosure of the Helium find in Japan, or its sale to Germany.

Germany also agreed to not disclose their access to a Helium supply. It would be necessary to transport liquid Helium since the Japanese freighter could hold only a fraction of the compressed gas volume necessary to fill a Zeppelin. Besides the empty returned gas bottles, the Japanese freighter would contain the components for a complete Helium gas liquefaction and processing plant, and a German engineer to oversee the installation.

Germany will provide all future liquid Helium transport, from the Port of Tomakomai, using freighters with large tanks built to transport liquid Helium.

The German Navy was underwriting most of the costs, since they wanted to adapt Hindenburg class airships to use as aircraft carriers. The carriers would hold at least 6 defensive fighters and 4 recon planes. The German Navy would use airship carriers to locate enemy convoys for submarine wolf packs. War is not yet on the horizon, but Britain is a recognizable threat. The airship would not be a threat to the Royal Navy, but in its recon role it would be faster, longer ranged, and less vulnerable than a ship based carrier.

A.G. Kimbrough

Mickey questioned the idea of using a much larger, offensive capable airship carrier. Goring wasn't interested, but he did support the Navy's plan, since most of the money to build the current in-design Graf Spee ship based carrier, would then be available for his aircraft development. He also agreed to start regular Lufthansa airship services between Japan and Germany, via New York, and Los Angeles.

With the agreement signed, Rio and Mickey spent the Christmas holidays at Heinrich's home, where Mickey met and fell in love with Heinrich's little sister, Gurti.

Rio returned home in January on the Japanese freighter to start producing the gas for the next shipment. Mickey was scheduled to spend over a year learning how to build airships, and Stuka dive bombers. He also planned to spend that year courting Gurti.

Eighteen-year-old Gurti was glad to be soon leaving her awkward teenage years. She had a quick wit she used to shield herself from the knowledge that she would never be called beautiful. Even though she was a head taller than this brash young man from Japan, she found him captivating, and romantic.

After an Austrian skiing trip where they made love for the first time Gurti agreed to return to Japan and become Mickey's wife.

A Different Approach Emerges

January, 1934

During Mickey's time at the Zeppelin factory, he concluded it would be impossible for Japan to produce an airship like the Hindenburg. The aluminum required would be more than would ever be available. The limited aluminum supply in Japan is not enough for the planned expansion of aircraft industry.

He cut short his training at the Zeppelin works and spent his last ten months in Germany considering an airship design using alternate materials that are more available in Japan.

He concluded that airship construction using the available bamboo and silk would be practical and have some advantages. The framing would be more complex, and would require glued joints, instead of rivets. The frame would bend instead of fracturing, when stressed, and silk for the outer cover and gas bags would be lighter and more tear resistant than the materials used on the Zeppelins.

He developed an airship carrier design concept that is three times larger than the Hindenburg class. This airship class would be capable of carrying three squadrons of fighters, torpedo bombers, and Stuka dive bombers, for a total of 90 combat aircraft. It would also carry fuel for over 5000 miles of cruising, at 100 miles per hour, and armaments and fuel for several full aircraft sorties.

He planned on using the Stuka dive bombers instead of the Japanese Navy's dive bomber. The Stuka is lighter, carried a heavier bomb load, and Mitsubishi would have the license to manufacture them. The Stuka had a shorter operating range than the Japanese plane, but the airship carrier mobility made that difference unimportant.

March 15, 1934

The soon to be a married couple and Gurti's mother take the first around the world flight of the Hindenburg.

Rio was waiting at the airfield for the Hindenburg, and his best friend's arrival. It would be a big occasion for the people of Japan, and a large crowd is present. Rio was in the VIP section, just behind the press. He noticed a blond Western woman with a large movie camera on a tripod. There is something familiar about her. Suddenly, he recognized Betty Lawrence.

Rio called out to her, and she turned, broke into a smile, and came over to him.

"I was hoping to see you while I was in Japan, but wasn't expecting to see you here."

Rio shared her smile, and said, "Both Mickey and Heinrich are on the Hindenburg. They're coming here for

After The Days Of Infamy

Mickey to get married to Heinrich's little sister. What are you doing here? I've been expecting to see you in the movies."

She replied, "I concluded I had no chance to become a star, so I went back to school, and now I work for Movietone News. I'm here to cover the Hindenburg's arrival in Japan. It sounds like I should also cover the wedding. Can you get me an invitation?"

"Of course, They will want you there, anyway. How long will you be in Japan?"

"I'm here to cover the Hindenburg's visit, but the next ship back to the states won't leave for another three weeks."

"Then I hope you will spend your free time with me, and I'll show you all the sights."

She smiled, and said, "I'll be busy until the Hindenburg departs, but I would love to see the sights with you, unless your wife objects."

Rio answered, "That won't be a problem, since I'm not married. I've just been too busy to get serious about finding someone."

Their conversation is interrupted by a rumble of crowd noise when the Hindenburg dropped out of the clouds.

Betty said, "Give me your phone number, and I'll call you the moment I'm free."

She blew him a kiss as she walked back to her camera.

The brief wedding ceremony is a mix of Buddhist and Catholic, and takes place during the Hindenburg's stopover in Tokyo with Rio, Betty, Gurti's mother, Heinrich present.

Mickey and Gurti move into his penthouse overlooking the bay. Mickey starts work on the new airship design at the

Mitsubishi Aircraft Design Center, and Gurti starts to build a life in Japan.

During the three weeks after the wedding, Rio and Betty made a grand tour of Japan's sights, and Inns, where their nights are filled with lovemaking. In the last week, Rio tried to bring up the subject of marriage. Betty said, "We're both too busy to consider that now."

They parted, promising to keep in touch with letters, until they could be together again.

August 15, 1934

Mickey's first objective is to sell the Mitsubishi Board on making a proposal to the Japanese military. That proposal calls for funding to build a prototype airship aircraft carrier. The fact his father was the majority stockholder, made Board approval for the proposal only a formality.

Mickey made a presentation to the Navy brass that included Admiral Isoroku Yamamoto, and Commander Minoru Genda. He showed a model of the under conversion Akagi aircraft carrier, and an identical scale model of the proposed airship carrier. The airship carrier model is almost three time the size of the Akagi model.

The conversion costs from a Battle Cruiser ship to a carrier ship are out of control. The cost estimates Mickey submitted for the prototype airship carrier, were less than the costs already expended on the Akagi conversion.

Two days later, the government authorized construction of a prototype airship. Because the project is classified Top Secret, the work would be done at a remote location. The remote location will prevent any Gaijin (non-Japanese) from ever sighting the airship.

After The Days Of Infamy

Because of that requirement, Mickey agreed to locate the production and operations facility at the Northern tip of Hokkaido Island, beside the Wakkanai Military Airbase.

December 3, 1934

The Airship project scale is immense and included construction of a hanger capable of holding two side-by-side airships. The prototype, designated ASC1, and is named Mount Fugi.

January 1935

The first shipment of liquid Helium is loaded on a new German liquid Helium tanker, and it departs for Homburg.

Rio is asked to join the government's Critical Materials Ministry, as the Director. He had been doing many of his father's duties in an unofficial capacity. But, with war approaching, the job became much more demanding.

Rio was spending three weeks of every month in Tokyo. He is pleased that Wade is running the Helium recovery and processing facilities. Wade frees him from needing to oversee those operations. The Helium sales to Germany are now generating a third of his companies profits.

Rio's father owned a British built yacht, the Sunflower. His father spent one summer sailing to Hawaii, and back, with the sixteen-year-old Rio as his sole companion. Rio frequently took the vessel sailing on his off week from Tokyo. Most of the time, he invited Wade and his bride to join him.

Occasionally, Mickey and Gurti would fly down and join them for the weekend. He had learned to fly in Germany and shipped back a prototype German Storch as his personal plane. Rio would fly with them when they planned to take the Sunflower out on an excursion.

Mickey is very busy overseeing the design and production of the Mt. Fugi and the Mitsubishi built Stuka dive bombers. The Navy resisted approving the German designed dive bomber over the Aichi D3A Navy standard dive bomber.

A prototype JU87 Stuka is delivered on the German liquid helium tanker. Then, a series of tests showed the Stuka to be clearly superior in bomb load capacity, and bombing precision. The Stuka did have a shorter operational range. Mickey made a strong case that the shorter range would not be a factor in airship carrier operations.

The Navy finally approved production of the Stuka, but continues production of the Aichi D3A for the aircraft carrier ships and land-based operations.

Mickey and his team did make some changes to the Stuka design. Those changes included incorporation of a Mitsubishi engine, folding wingtips, and a tail hook. The changes and production development for the Stuka would not result in full production until early 1941.

After his father died, Rio had the Sunflower overhauled and made like new.

By the time the processing plant was ready to ship processed gas, Rio's father had suffered a stroke, and Rio has to assume his father's Ministerial responsibilities. He realized that he must convince Wade to continue running the Helium operations. He knew Wade is planning to return to the states and had sold the drilling rig to his foreman. The rig and drilling crew will depart, to join an offshore drilling operation, as soon as the last Helium well is completed.

After The Days Of Infamy

Rio discovers an unexpected ally in his quest to have Wade keep running the Helium Processing operations. His ally becomes the daughter of the innkeeper where Wade is living.

Wade had grown tired of the cramped conditions of living on site in the office trailer. Since this assignment would be long term, he resolved to find more comfortable living quarters. Three miles North of the drilling site is the village of Takinoue. There is a 200-year-old inn, which caters to visitors to a local Buddhist shrine.

Wade is elated to find that the largest suite contains a Western style toilet. He had managed the "traditional" facilities, but they are far from comfortable, or private. When he inquired about the bathing facilities, the owner showed him a room down the hall from his suite. It contains a large wooden tub and an enclosed shower at the entrance. The owner told him the water is heated an hour after the end of the evening meal.

Wade negotiated a price for the suite and paid the next month's rent in advance.

On the first day, he is ten minutes late returning from the drill site, and dinner is already on the table. There were only two other guests. They are an older couple, who speak no English. He finished his dinner, which included two containers of hot Saki.

The owner had been careful to explain that Wade should shower before entering the soaking tub. He dug out the bathrobe that had been his fathers, undressed, put it on, and walked down the hall.

He had just finished his shower and was walking over to the tub when he noticed the owner and his family, including his teenage daughter, already in the tub. Everyone was in a similar state of undress, and all Wade could do was mumble a greeting and climb in.

Already aware of the Japanese casual attitude toward nudity, he still had a hard time keeping his eyes off of the young lady, who the owner introduced as his daughter, Hekoi.

A few minutes later the older couple joined the party, and Wade had to move over, closer to Hekoi.

She had about the same amount of English as Wade had Japanese, but both attempted to communicate. Soon the water started to cool. The older couple left first, then Hekoi's parents, and shortly after they left, Hekoi pointed to the goose bumps on her breasts and climbed out of the tub, giggling. Wade waited until she left the room before climbing out of the tub. By then, he was shaking from the chilling water. As he reached for his robe, Hekoi reappeared, still naked, and holding a large towel.

As she handed it to him, she looked down and noticed the developing erection he had worked unsuccessfully, to suppress all evening. She gasped, put her hand over her mouth, and giggled again.

Wade grabbed the towel and used it to cover his privates. She took one end of the towel and started to dry his back. In the process, her breasts brushed his arm, she gasped again, jumped away, and the towel fell to the floor.

Wade now has a full blown erection and her nipples are extended. For a few seconds, they just stare. Then Hekoi smiled and touched his penis. Wade cupped a breast in his hand. The moment lasted a few seconds, before both step back. Wade reached for his robe and Hekoi picked up the towel, wrapped it around her, and left the room.

Over the next months the couple worked together on

their respective languages, and both improve. Their mutual attraction grew, and Wade knew it was only a matter of time before they made love. He confessed his concern to Rio, who brought him a box of rubbers from Tokyo.

Hekoi's parents are not unaware of their daughters developing love affair, and take no action. She came to his room one night in May and they made love. It became a regular practice, and Wade was thinking about proposing to her. But her family would not permit it, if he would take her away from Japan. Wade agreed to continue managing the Helium Operations for the duration of the five year well commission period.

September 15, 1934

Wade and Hekoi married and spent a week in Tokyo on their honeymoon. On their last evening in Tokyo, Rio took them to a lavish meal at one the best restaurants, where Mickey and Gurti joined them.

During the meal, Hekoi asked Rio why he has not found a girl friend. Rio explained that his true love is a news reel reporter for Movietone News, and their separate careers keep them apart. He closed the conversation by saying he hoped one day for to her to marry him.

When the couple returned, Wade discovered that his father-in-law did not give him a discount on the suite, even though he was now renting Hekoi's former room.

February 12,1935

Lt. Jg. Jason Jared (JJ) Wycliff is a fighter pilot assigned to the Airship Carrier Macon on the night of the crash. When it became clear, the airship is going down, the Captain orders the launch of the Sparrowhawk fighter to direct rescue ships to the crash location.

Lt. Jg. Wycliff is in command of the fighter squadron and insisted he fly the plane, even though the Macon was going down at a steeper angle than the trapeze had ever been deployed. It took extra seconds for the six foot six inch tall Wycliff to climb into the tight cockpit.

As the trapeze lowered the Sparrowhawk, the airship angle increased, and the weight of the plane caused the hoist to bind up, and stop, half-way down. Wycliff could not release the Sparrowhawk. The impact with the water tore the trapeze and plane loose, just before the Macon crashed on top of them.

Somehow Wycliff was in the water and being pulled into a life raft.

Wycliff woke five days later in the San Diego Naval hospital, with a concussion, a broken arm, and a shattered collarbone.

His wife Veronica, was a Philadelphia debutante from old money. She fell for him during his last year at the Naval Academy.

Veronica took the train from their apartment in Northern California to be near him. She stayed at a suite in the Hotel Coronado. Although those rooms are limited to high level Officers, her father's DC connections insured a place was waiting for her.

When Wycliff woke, he became enraged when he found where she is staying, at a cost he could never afford. Their fights had increased in numbers and intensity over the years, and this one culminated in Veronica returning home to Philadelphia. They parted, agreeing to write, and did so, intermittently.

After The Days Of Infamy

November 16, 1935

Eight months, and six operations later, Wycliffe received orders to report to Washington for a temporary assignment. He called Veronica from the San Diego train station and asked her to meet him in DC. She met him at the station, and tearfully insisted that they should stay together, always.

The next morning Wycliff reported to a BuPers Captain and is told that his days as a fighter pilot are finished. His damaged collarbone could not withstand combat Gee forces, or the shock of carrier landings. While he kept his wings, his options are limited to accepting a medical discharge, or continue flying either transports, or blimps. There was even a concern about the shock of rough water landings that would prevent him from flying float planes, or flying boats.

The thought of only being able to fly C 47s was not appealing, so he chose to fly blimps. The Captain told him to talk it over with his wife and come back in the morning to sign the papers after thinking about it overnight.

The discharge option delighted Veronica since her father had a place waiting for him in his Brokerage House. She became enraged when he refused to consider it. The next morning he signed the papers, checked out of the hotel and took the train to his new duty station at Lakehurst New Jersey. Veronica returned to Philadelphia and filed divorce papers.

Wycliff was already qualified as a bridge Officer on the Macon, so after a few months training he is promoted to Lieutenant, and in command of a blimp.

A.G. Kimbrough

October 15, 1937

After the first flight operations of the Mount Fugi were flawless, the approvals for the next three airships are issued, a week later, by Commander Minoru Genda. He said the Akagi would be the last Carrier ship built by Japan. The next three airships are due for completion by June 1941.

August 17, 1938

Commander Wallace Anderson, a Materials Engineer assigned to NAVSHIPS finally gained approval for the evaluation of a revolutionary alternative to conventional Battleship Armor.

Corning Glass developed a ceramic armor that promised to save weight and costs over conventional steel armor plate. They had tried, without success, to sell it to the Army, but the Army considered it too unproven, and too late, to adapt for the Sherman tank design.

Corning warmed over their Army proposal for the Navy Battleships, to use three, three inch thick ceramic plates, stacked together, with rubber pads between them.

Anderson's boss considered the project a waste of time, because everyone knew ceramic armor would never be a match for steel armor. However, Commander Anderson had run the numbers, and that is why he is willing to risk his career on the test program.

He spent six months and all of his personal credibility fighting to get the test approved. If the ceramic armor did not look promising, he probably would be forced into early retirement.

A Gathering of War Clouds

October, 1938

The conflict between the Republic of China and the Empire of Japan begins.

November 26, 1938

The morning was cold at the Dahlgren, Virginia Naval Gun Test Range, when Commander Anderson climbed the steps to the Range Control Tower. Below him, a Navy crew was getting the single 16"/50 gun ready for the tests. The gun was identical with the nine planned for the new Fast Battleship Class being designed. A trailer behind the gun held 20 standard armor piercing projectiles, and a second trailer held 20 powder canisters.

A.G. Kimbrough

Positioned 10,000 yards down range, were a pair of Battleship hull mock-ups. One, 20 foot wide mock-up had the same 11 inch thick Class B armor plate planned for use on the first ship in the Fast Battleship Class the USS Iowa, BB61.

Although the second mock-up had the same internal structure as the first, it employed the ceramic armor, comprised of three overlapping layers of three inch thick cast ceramic plate, with half inch thick rubber pads between the ceramic plates.

The Performance Test called for the gun to fire ten, 2700 pound armor piercing projectiles, at each mock-up. Alternate targets would be hit with every shell. High speed movie cameras would record each shell's impact.

Corning's Project Engineer and Project Manager were in the Control Tower with Commander Anderson. But, other than the Range Safety Officer, no other Officer, even those from his group were willing to observe the test.

Everyone knew there would be a failure of the "glass" armour. No one wanted to have their reputation and promotion prospects besmirched by that failure.

Those present watched the impacts with long range optics from the Control Tower. Other than the smoke and dust, not much could be determined from the shell hits.

After the last shell impacted, and the All Clear flags went up, Commander Anderson and the guys from Corning climbed into a jeep and rode down range.

Standard armor plate mock-up damage matched earlier tests, with only minor penetration where multiple shells impacted in the same place.

The ceramic plate mock-up showed cracks and the

outer plates shattered, where single shells impacted. Two outer plates were shattered when impacted by two shells. All three plates shattered where multiple shells impacted within a twelve-inch circle. However, the penetration of the quarter inch thick backup plate was similar to that experienced on the armor plate mock-up.

While multiple hits within a twelve-inch circle damaged the inside plate, the internal damage was the same as occurred on the standard armour plate under the same conditions.

The reality of naval main battery combat made the possibility of multiple hits within a small area infinitesimal. Anything better than a five percent main battery hit rate is considered exceptional.

The Corning guys are ecstatic. The Project Engineer pulls out a flag, and waves it to the occupants of a six by six truck beside the blockhouse. It arrived at the mock-up five minutes later, and two guys pulled off the damaged tiles. Four hours later, the broken tiles are replaced, and the mock-up is restored to its pretest condition.

The test results created a bombshell at Navships, with several very senior Officers changing their stance on Ceramic Armor.

January 8, 1939

After Commander Anderson circulated a report outlining the advantages of Ceramic Armor over steel armor, that included:

Equal impact performance,

An 80% armor weight savings,

The 30% savings in construction time,

The ability for the crew to repair battle damage at sea, using on-board spares, and,

Saving enough construction costs, to pay for an Atlanta Class Light Cruiser.

Within a week after the report is circulated, the initial design for the Iowa is changed to incorporate Ceramic Armor.

The new design for the Iowa predicted a top speed increase to 38 knots, because of the armor weight reduction.

September, 1939

With the German invasion of Poland, World War Two begins.

Within hours of the British declaration of War, the "Battle of the Atlantic" starts with the sinking of a liner by the German submarine, U30. Within days, the entire German submarine fleet is at sea, accompanied by a pair of Zeppelin Aircraft Carriers. The effects of this combined force of wolf-packs directed by scout planes based on the airships, decimates any convoys headed for the United Kingdom.

September 17, 1939

Aircraft carrier HMS Courageous is torpedoed and sunk by U-29 on patrol off the coast of Ireland.

After The Days Of Infamy

October 14, 1939

The battleship, UMS Royal Oak is anchored at Scapa Flow in Orkney, Scotland, when she is torpedoed and sunk by the German submarine U-47.

February, 1940

The Japanese Diet announces a record high budget with over half its expenditures being for the military.

March, 1940

Meat rationing starts in Britain, as the effects of the submarine blockade reaches crises levels.

Japan has changed for the worse in many ways. The Military is now in absolute control, and a high level of paranoia against all Gaijin is far-flung. Shortages in raw materials and manufacturing capacity are widespread. The special tank cars used to transport the liquid Helium became hard to obtain, and the Navy has commandeered every new one available.

The shipboard plumbing system used to fill and unload the liquid Helium tanks are complex, and the Captain of the second German tanker had to hire an engineer to oversee that system's operation and maintenance. He could not find a German willing to join his crew, even at top wages. He finally hired a Dutchman, who had been working in the German Merchant Marine for several years. Since his wife was German, and they lived in Hamburg, the German security officers approved his access to the Secret Helium transport project.

A.G. Kimbrough

April 18, 1940

The next shipment of liquid Helium was ready to depart Japan. On the morning before the scheduled departure, Rio received a call from the ship's Captain. When he told Rio that the Kempeitai Secret Police had arrested his Dutch engineer, Rio promised to look into the matter.

His call to the headquarters of the Secret Police reviled that they were arresting all non German Gaijin who had access to the Helium project. The call shook him to the bone, because he knew they would come for Wade. He called Mickey and asked him to fly him home, with great discretion.

They met at the airport within an hour, and Rio explained the situation. Mickey agreed, since Wade was also his friend and the Kempeitai were possibly in route. Depending on which ferry they caught, their trip would take at least eight hours.

Two hours later, the Storch touched down on a grass field by Rio's home. They drove the caretaker's car to the processing plant and alerted Wade. When they explained his danger he agreed that he must escape immediately, or face certain imprisonment. Rio told him to take the Sunflower and sail to Hawaii. Wade followed them back to the inn for a quick stop.

Wade's initial reaction was to leave Hekoi with her family until it was safe for her to join him in the states. She flatly refused, and reminded him it would take two people to sail the Sunflower. Her parents were not pleased, but recognized the danger that Hekoi would face if she remained in Japan. After packing a few things, Wade tossed his truck keys to his father-in-law and the couple left with Rio and Mickey.

After The Days Of Infamy

Rio and Mickey returned to Tokyo after dropping the Callahans off at the marina where the Sunflower is berthed. They arrived, just before sundown, at the small suburban airport where Mickey kept the Storch.

Wade used a tire iron to break the lock on the gate to the Sunflower's berth. He replaced it, so it is not obviously broken, and prepared for their voyage. The fuel tanks were always full, and Wade filled the water tanks.

They motored out of the marina and left the harbor under the light of the moon. Rio warned him not to run South through the Inland Sea, since an air search could find them. The run North would be much longer, and subject to a lot rougher weather, but they would be less likely to be detected.

Rio was in his Tokyo office the next afternoon when the Kempeita arrived. The four men spent the afternoon interrogating him about Wade Callahan. Rio stuck with the story, that as far as he knew, Wade was at work at the Helium Processing Plant on Hokado.

The next morning, the same team returned and demanded to know if he knew the Sunflower was missing. He replied that he had hosted the Callahans on a few sailing excursion around the island, but he did not understand why Wade would steal his boat.

The Sunflower sailed due North until they were close to Russian waters, before turning East. They only used the sails, since their fuel was not sufficient for the distance they must travel. Wade only ran the engine for an hour each day to charge the batteries for the radio and the bilge pump.

Since their food supplies are limited to a hundred pound of rice and a pantry full of canned food, they fish every day with mixed results. The winds were favorable, but after the second week, the sea got rougher. By the third week, the seas required them to reduce sail, and run under the jib. The pounding seas kept them sore, wet, and uncomfortable.

May, 1940

Germany invaded Belgium, France, Luxembourg and the Netherlands; Winston Churchill becomes Prime Minister of the United Kingdom after Neville Chamberlain resigned.

May 21, 1940

In the predawn morning, a rogue wave rolled over the Sunflower. Hekoi was at the helm, and is smashed against the cockpit, breaking her forearm, and giving her a concussion. The same wave splintered the foremast, swept away most of the rigging, and almost capsized the boat. Wade spent the next 24 hours in a frantic effort to treat Hekoi, deploy a sea anchor, and clear away the wreckage.

It took another week before he could get a jury rigged sail set, and start moving toward their destination at three knots.

He continued to turn on the radio each evening, but the shortened antenna produced mostly static.

June 3,1940

The Allied evacuation of 340,000 troops from Dunkirk is complete.

During the evacuation, a Messerschmidt 109 is hit by antiaircraft fire, and crashes just offshore. The Pilot, Rolf Craiger is killed. He is a boyhood friend of Heinrich, who was his Best Man when he married a Spanish girl, Maria Delgado, at the end of the War in Spain.

June 4, 1940

Rolf Craiger's Squadron Commander had also been at his wedding, and knew Heinrich. He didn't want Maria to get the news from a telegram. He called Heinrich, and asked him to tell her, since she had no family in Germany.

Heinrich had maintained contact with Rolf and Maria, and saw them whenever he was in Berlin. He flew there, and knocked on her door just before sundown.

Maria was still in her uniform, having just completed her shift as an Emergency Room nurse.

She saw Heinrich's grim expression, and spoke, "It's Rolf, isn't it?"

Heinrich spent the evening trying to comfort her. When she finally went to sleep, he spent the night on a chair in her living room. The next morning, he offered to fly her back to Madrid, so she could be with her family, but she insisted on staying in Berlin to work at the hospital. It was receiving a steady stream of war casualties and her skills are needed. Heinrich promised to stay in touch, and urged her to call any time she needed his help.

June 14, 1940

That evening, a strong signal broke through the static. It was a tanker bound for Hawaii, inquiring about dock space at Pearl Harbor. Wade's distress call is quickly answered, and an hour later, the tanker came into view. Since Hekoi did not require immediate emergency medical attention, Wade asked the tanker to relay a request for a tug to meet them and give them a tow into the harbor.

A.G. Kimbrough

The next morning he is surprised to see a Coast Guard Cutter with the tug. The cutter followed them into the harbor, and was at the dock when the Sunflower approached it. An officer, with two armed seaman came aboard, and asked if he was Wade Callahan. When he said yes, the officer told him he was under arrest on an international warrant, for the theft of the Sunflower, and the murder of it's owner.

After they cuffed him, Wade told the office to look in the strongbox under the deck plates of the main cabin. Then the officer found two documents in the strongbox. He found the first document was a bill of sale for the Sunflower from Rio to Wade Callahan for the sum of $10,000 US. He then found the second document was a letter, signed by both Rio and Mickey, which stated that these two men helped Mr. Callahan escape a witch-hunt by the Military secret police. The letter also requested the authorities to not disclose its contents to any Japanese authorities, since such a disclosure would lead to both their deaths at the hands of the same secret police.

After consulting overnight with the State Department in Washington, Wade and Hekoi are released, with a suggestion they return to the states as soon as possible. The message from State warned that the island had many people that were agents of the Japanese government. Wade signed the paperwork to have the tug company sell the Sunflower, pay the fees with the proceeds, and wire the remaining funds to his Barclay's Bank account.

After a doctor's visit, where Hekoi had a cast put on her arm, the couple checked into a good hotel, and planned to spend the next two weeks relaxing and enjoying the island before boarding the next Pan Am Clipper to San Francisco.

However, the next morning, Wade received a call from

44

the tug captain, who reported a closing time visit from two tough looking Japs They demanded to know the whereabouts of Mr. Callahan. He didn't disclose their location, and they left. Wade thanked him and decided to leave the islands immediately.

June 19th, 1940

A call to a travel agent revealed that there was only one passenger ship leaving before the clipper. Unfortunately, the liner is booked, with no cabins available.

Wade went down to the ship to see if there was any alternatives, such as steerage passage to the next port. Even after handing the Purser a hundred dollar bill, he is informed that they did not offer steerage passage, and the Purser could suggest no other alternative.

As Wade left the Purser's office, he overheard a couple in the hall outside talking. They are going to see if they could cancel their booked passage, since they wanted to spend more time on the island. Wade was waiting for them as they left the ship. When the couple reached the dock, Wade struck up a conversation with them. He found out their refund request had been refused by the Purser. Wade offered to exchange cash equal to the Clipper tickets costs for their ship tickets, and they accepted his offer.

The couple's luggage was tagged, ready to be delivered to the ship that afternoon, and after they said they could empty the big chest, Wade bought it. That afternoon Wade picked up the big chest in a taxi, and put the new clothes Hekoi purchased for them that morning inside. Then the couple took the taxi to the ship and boarded early. The ship departed the islands at midnight. There was a disturbance just before departure, when two Jap thugs tried to board the ship.

Wade and Hekoi found the liner a luxurious change from the Sunflower. The weather was warmer, their accommodations comfortable, and the food excellent. There were hours every day with time for reading, enjoying the pool, and just recovering in spirit and physically. The passage through the Panama Canal was fascinating.

The ship's only scheduled stop, was a day excursion in Havana before the ship was due to arrive the following morning at Miami.

As the ship started through the Caribbean, the couple grew concerned that Japanese agents might be waiting for them at the dock when they arrived in Miami.

The couple left the ship in Havana, carrying only a small bag. Wade left two hundred dollars with the Purser to mark their return before the ship departed that evening. He also composed a suicide note and left it in their cabin.

The note stated that the couple could not stand the thought of being sent back to Japan, or spending the rest of their lives on the run, so they would end it together by jumping overboard during the night.

They walked to the other side of the waterfront and hired a fishing boat to take them to a small village fifty miles up the coast. They rented a small house that overlooked the water, and started a new chapter in the rest of their lives. The couple would take a bus to Havana once a month and buy what they needed, that was not available in the village. Usually, Wade would buy any recent US papers that were available.

July 1940

Surveillance of Rio had stopped. The Kempeita could not make a strong enough case against an important minister, and there were other higher priorities for their resources and time.

The operations and training of the Airship fleet was continuing at a high level off the North end of Hokkaido Island, where there was no chance for a foreign national to catch sight of them.

President Roosevelt asked Congress for huge increases in military preparations.

Fumimaro Konoye is named the Prime Minister of Japan.

August, 1940

Herman Goring starts a two-week assault on British airfields to prepare for invasion, and the "Battle of Britain" begins. The British defensive efforts are hampered by the shortages resulting from the convoy blockade. The population is also living with many shortages and severe rationing.

British scientist Sir Henry Tizard leaves for the United States on the Tizard Mission, giving to the Americans several top secret British technologies. They include the magnetron, the secret device at the heart of radar, which is already proving itself in the defense of Britain.

August 16, 1940

A first draft of the Destroyers for Bases Agreement by the US and Britain is made public. There is a large scale objection to this agreement by many in the American public.

A.G. Kimbrough

August 18, 1940

After heavy bomber losses, Hitler stops the air raids on Britain, declaring that he wants peace with the British people. The proclamation also stated that the convoy blockade will continue until the British people depose of the warmongers in their government.

August 20, 1940

Churchill's speech "Never was so much owed by so many to so few" is delivered to the House of Commons. It is not accepted by everyone.

September 2, 1940

The Destroyers for Bases Agreement is voted down after a bitter congressional debate.

September 3, 1940

Hitler announces a postponement of the invasion of Britain, to give the British people more time to consider peace. The convoy blockade will continue. However, the failure of the Destroyers for Bases Agreement and fears of the forthcoming invasion continue to haunt Britain. The pressure on the Government is immense, and increasing every day.

October 30. 1940

President Roosevelt, in the middle of an election campaign, promises not to send "our boys" to war. His popularity, because of the opposition to the failed Destroyers for Bases Agreement had fallen, and this statement was an attempt to defuse that opposition.

After The Days Of Infamy

November 5, 1940

President Roosevelt wins a third term, by only the narrowest of margins, and Britain's hopes for more American support are dashed.

November 11, 1940

British naval forces launch an attack against the Italian navy at Taranto. Swordfish bombers from HMS Illustrious damage three battleships, two cruisers and multiple auxiliary craft.. The event fails to secure British supply lines in the Mediterranean. The British initial success with airborne shallow water torpedos is studied by the Japanese military already preparing for an attack on Pearl Harbor.

November 13, 1940

Molotov meets Hitler again, asking acceptance of a Russian plan to liquidate Finland. Hitler now resists every attempt to expand Soviet influence in Europe. He sees Britain as defeated and offers India to the Soviet Union.

December 1, 1940

President Roosevelt asked Joseph P. Kennedy, the US Ambassador to the United Kingdom, to resign. Kennedy gave a newspaper interview expressing the view that "Democracy is finished in England". Kennedy believes that Churchill used his friendship with Roosevelt to have him fired, and stays in London to finance a continuous political war to unseat Churchill.

The USS Iowa, BB-61 is laid down under an accelerated construction program.

A.G. Kimbrough

December 16, 1940

Since Germany stopped bombing Britain, the RAF has made no flights over Germany or France. But, the this night the RAF makes a large raid on Mannheim, Germany.

The following night, the German Air Force launches a massive raid on London that Kills 263 civilians. Kennedy leads the outcry, with a full-page cartoon of Churchill's bloody hands, demanding that he keep the RAF out of Germany to avoid killing his own people. It ran on the front page of every major paper in Britain, and achieved the desired results. The RAF did not return to Germany or France and Hitler did not retaliate again.

Churchill tried to have Kennedy thrown out of Britain for inciting the people against the government, but the attempt failed.

December 18, 1940

Hitler issues a directive to begin planning for the German invasion of the Soviet Union.

January 10, 1941

Germany and Italy now have both aircraft and naval supremacy in the Mediterranean, and the only support for Britain's North African forces must come overland through Egypt. Their offense against Tobruk stalls.

January 23, 1941

The Royal Navy Carrier, HMS Illustrious, is heavily damaged by air attacks and leaves Malta for repairs in Alexandria. It is sunk by German submarines while in route.

After The Days Of Infamy

February 1, 1941

Admiral Husband Kimmel is appointed the Commander of the US Navy in the Pacific.

February 11, 1941

Elements of the Afrika Korps start to arrive in Tripoli.

March 10, 1941

Lt. Jg. Elmer Price, joines the pre-commissioning crew of the USS Fletcher as her Gunnery Officer. Price is a Mustang, an officer who formally was an enlisted man. He had been a Chief Fire Controlman, who specialized in radar controlled fire control systems.

March 24, 1941

Rommel attacks and reoccupies El Agheila, Libya in his first offensive. The British retreat and within three weeks are driven back to Egypt.

April 12, 1941

Japan and the Soviet Union sign a neutrality pact, and Hitler is not pleases when he hears that news, since it could allow the Soviet forces in the far East to return to the West.

May 9, 1941

A Japanese brokered peace treaty signed in Tokyo ends the French-Thai War.

May 24, 1941

British Battleship HMS Hood is sunk in the North

Atlantic, by a powerful salvo from German battleship Bismark. The salvo is fired from extreme range. While the Hood's side armour is very heavy, the deck armour is too thin to resist the downward plunging amour-piercing shells of the Bismark, which detonate the main battery magazines.

June 22, 1941

Germany invades the Soviet Union with Operation Barbarossa, a three-pronged operation aimed at Leningrad, Moscow, and the southern oil fields of the Caucasus. This action ends the Molotov-Ribbentrop Pact. Romania invades the South-Western border areas of the Soviet Union, on the side of Germany.

June 29, 1941

When the fourth Japanese Airship is completed, the Naval Airship branch goes on a war footing, with intensive training in shallow water torpedo attacks, and Stuka Dive Bomber attacks on ship targets.

July 26, 1941

In response to the Japanese occupation of French Indochina, US President Roosevelt orders the seizure of all Japanese assets in the United States.

July 31, 1941

Hitler orders SS general Reinhard Heydrich to "submit a general plan of the administrative material and financial measures necessary for carrying out the desired Final Solution of the Jewish question."

The Japanese naval ministry accuses the United States

of intruding into their territorial waters at Sukumo Bay, and then fleeing. Japan offers no evidence to prove this allegation.

August 1, 1941

The US announces an oil embargo against "aggressors."

August 20, 1941

Winston Churchill is defending his government's war policies, on the floor of Parliament when he suffers a massive heart attack, and dies. His death throws the government into a battle between hard liners and those seeking peace with Germany, and an end to the blockade.

September 11, 1941

A historic Parliament vote directs the Government to seek a Peace Agreement with Germany.

When the news is announced, the German Foreign Office broadcast the following message:

"The people of Germany have no desire to be at war with our English Brothers. We know the hardships the blockade has forced on you. We will have representatives at our Lisbon Embassy, ready to discuss a meaningful agreement to end all hostilities, within the week."

September 30, 1941

The treaty is signed by representatives of both countries. It will become effective after:

- The United Kingdom declared complete Neutrality,

- All UK Military forces stand down and cease all hostilities,

- All Royal Navy Capital ships enter a German Controlled Port, and surrender to the authorities there, or be scuttled outside their home ports,

- All Royal Air Force combat aircraft parked, out of shelters, at their bases,

- The German Military will do a visual inspection of the ships and will take custody of aircraft and all overseas military hardware,

- Any Ship or combat aircraft found in violation of this Treaty after October 30, 1941 will be destroyed, and the crews considered war criminals.

- When these actions are completed, the blockade will be lifted, and normal, peaceful relations, include equitable trade, will be established.

October 8,1941

Toshie Kihara was a Japanese American journalist, who graduated from UCLA in 1935. She had worked for the LA Times since graduation. Betty Laurence interviewed her on film shortly after she is fired, following an outcry over her writing an article warning that the potential new Tojo government would likely start a war with the United States. The voices demanding her firing included Japanese-Americans loyal to Japan and those businessmen who were making lots of money trading with Japan. Betty is impressed with Toshie's grasp of current events and her writing abilities.

Because of Betty's strong recommendations, Toshie is hired as a copywriter for Movietone News in Los Angeles.

After The Days Of Infamy

October 10, 1941

In a direct violation of orders, Admiral Andrew Cunningham leads most of the Royal Navy fleet out of Scapa Flow, in a twilight start of a dash across the North Atlantic to Canada. Zeppelin Carrier directed wolf-packs sink a third of the fleet. All ships were flying Canadian Flags as they left Scapa Flow.

German armies encircle about 660,000 Red Army troops near Vyasma (east of Smolensk); and some make a glowing prediction of the end of the war.

The British Army in North Africa retreats to Egypt and establishes a defensive line at El Alamein under a Canadian flag.

October 15, 1941

Roosevelt announces that some Naval Construction programs have been expedited.

October 16,1941

The Soviet Union's government begins to move Eastward to Samara, a city on the Volga, but Stalin remains in Moscow. The citizens of Moscow frantically build tank traps and other fortifications for the coming siege.

October 17,1941

Japanese prime minister Prince Fumimaro Konove's government collapses, leaving little hope for peace in the Pacific. Both Mickey and Rio had been secretly supporting the Prince hoping to avoid war. They agree to keep a low political profile to avoid the developing purge by the Army leaders under Tojo.

A.G. Kimbrough

October 18,1941

Red Army troop reinforcements arrive in Moscow from Siberia; Stalin is assured that the Japanese will not attack the USSR from the East.

General Hideki Tojo becomes the 40th Prime Minister of Japan.

October 29, 1941

Canada, Australia, India, South Africa, and New Zealand declare their complete independence from Britain. All five nations offer to sign a Mutual Defense Treaty with the United States.

October 31,1941

Germany announces that the terms of the treaty are satisfied, and that the blockade of the United Kingdom is lifted. The German inspection teams arrive in London to complete the combat aircraft survey, and disable or remove the aircraft. They find that all of the British Combat aircraft are disabled. The survey team sets them on fire and returns home.

November 1, 1941

President Roosevelt announces that the U.S. Coast Guard is now be under the direction of the U.S. Navy, a transition of authority usually reserved only for wartime.

November 6, 1941

Stalin addresses the Soviet Union for only the second time during his three-decade rule. He states that even though 350,000 troops are killed in German attacks so far, the Germans have lost 4.5 million soldiers (a gross exaggeration) and that Soviet victory is near.

November 15, 1941

Two Airship support ships depart Japan for a point in the North Pacific that is 1500 miles Northeast of Hawaii.

November 17, 1941

The United States ambassador to Japan, cables the State Department that he expects Japan has plans to launch an attack against Pearl Harbor, Hawaii.

November 26.1941

The United States delivers the Hull Note ultimatum to Japan.

The repatriation of Prisoners Of War, starts between Germany and Britain.

With the end of the blockade, the four German Airship carriers return to the Zeppelin works, for modifications to carry Stuka dive-bombers. The airships will remain under the command of now-Admiral Dönitz, but the Stukas and pilots will be under the command of Goering whenever the airships are assigned to a special mission.

December 2,1941

Prime Minister Tojo rejects "peace feelers" from the US.

December 4,1941

Japanese naval and army forces continue to move

toward Southeast Asia.

December 5, 1941

Germans halt the attack on Moscow, now with the front only eleven miles away when the USSR counter-attacks during a heavy blizzard.

The Airship Fleet leaves the Wakkanai Military Airbase for Pearl Harbor.

Days of Infamy

December 7, 1941, 0740:

The leading elements of the 320 plane Strike Force are approaching from the Southwest and have Pearl Harbor in sight. The open radio transmission of "Tora Tora Tora" indicates that the surprise is complete.

December 7, 1941, 1110:

The Strike Force returns after achieving a devastating success. Aircraft losses are less than expected. Several Battleships are burning and sunk. Refueling and re-arming the Strike Force begins.

A.G. Kimbrough

December 7, 1941, 1450:

The Strike Force departs on the second strike.

December 7, 1941, 1720:

Captain Minoru Genda smiled as the last plane landed on the Kaga. Both attacks have succeeded beyond his wildest expectations. The second strike had not even lost a single plane. The losses on the first attack were even less than projected.

As the four carriers turned, he could see the smoke, rising over the burning ships and oil storage tanks. Even from 50 miles away, and at an 8,000 foot altitude, he could see that the smoke column height was way above his vantage point on the carrier bridge.

December 8, 1941, 0945:

The airship fleet stopped above their support ships, a 1000 miles West of Portland Oregon. Each of the two support ships is a large freighter with a hundred foot tall mast on the bow. Each carrier airship will, connect to the top of the mast, to resupply fuel, armaments, and replacement planes. The carrier airship fleet will bring destruction to the American West Coast before the end of the week.

December 8, 1941, 1230:

President Roosevelt addressed a joint secession of Congress.

"Mr. Vice President, Mr. Speaker, Members of the House of Representatives:

"Yesterday, December 7th, 1941 ~ a date which will live

in infamy ~ the United States of America was suddenly and deliberately attacked by naval and air forces of the Empire of Japan.

"The United States was at peace with that nation and, at the solicitation of Japan, was still in conversation with its government and its emperor looking toward the maintenance of peace in the Pacific.

"Indeed, one hour after Japanese air squadrons had commenced bombing in the American island of Oahu, the Japanese ambassador to the United States and his colleague delivered to our Secretary of State a formal reply to a recent American message. And while this reply stated that it seemed useless to continue the existing diplomatic negotiations, it contained no threat or hint of war or of armed attack.

"It will be recorded that the distance of Hawaii from Japan makes it obvious that the attack was deliberately planned many days or even weeks ago. During the intervening time, the Japanese government has deliberately sought to deceive the United States by false statements and expressions of hope for continued peace.

"The attack yesterday on the Hawaiian islands has caused severe damage to American naval and military forces. I regret to tell you that very many American lives have been lost. In addition, American ships have been reported torpedoed on the high seas between San Francisco and Honolulu.

"Yesterday, the Japanese government also launched an attack against Malaya.

"Last night, Japanese forces attacked Hong Kong.

"Last night, Japanese forces attacked Guam.

A.G. Kimbrough

"Last night, Japanese forces attacked the Philippine Islands.

"Last night, the Japanese attacked Wake Island.

"And this morning, the Japanese attacked Midway Island.

"Japan has, therefore, undertaken a surprise offensive extending throughout the Pacific area. The facts of yesterday and today speak for themselves. The people of the United States have already formed their opinions and well understand the implications to the very life and safety of our nation.

"As Commander-in-chief of the Army and Navy, I have directed that all measures be taken for our defense. But always will our whole nation remember the character of the onslaught against us.

"No matter how long it may take us to overcome this premeditated invasion, the American people in their righteous might will win through to absolute victory.

"I believe that I interpret the will of the Congress and of the people when I assert that we will not only defend ourselves to the uttermost, but will make it very certain that this form of treachery shall never again endanger us.

"Hostilities exist. There is no blinking at the fact that our people, our territory, and our interests are in grave danger.

"With confidence in our armed forces, with the unbending determination of our people, we will gain the inevitable triumph ~ so help us God.

"I ask that the Congress declare that since the unprovoked and dastardly attack by Japan on Sunday, December 7th, 1941, a state of war has existed between the

United States and the Japanese empire."

Within an hour, the German Ambassador delivered an official note to the White House that expresses dismay at the Japanese attack on Pearl Harbor, and the strongest desire to maintain normal, peaceful relations with the United States.

Later, the United States, Canada, Australia, India, the Netherlands and New Zealand declare war on Japan.

The failure of Germany to join their Declaration of War against the United States is a surprise to the Japanese Government because it represents a reversal of their earlier position.

Japanese forces take the Gilbert Islands. Clark Field in the Philippines is bombed, and many American aircraft are destroyed on the ground.

December 10, 1941

British Battleship HMS Repulse and the battleship HMS Prince of Wales are sunk in a Japanese air attack in the South China Sea.

December 11, 1941, 0815:

The Commander of the Navy Yard Puget Sound in Bremerton, Washington finally got a telephone connection with his boss in Washington DC. They resume a discussion on the logistics necessary for the yard to shift from a primary new construction roll, to repair of the ships damaged at Pearl Harbor.

The 320 plane Japanese Strike Force passes over the crest of the Olympic mountains and splits into two groups. One group has an equal mix of torpedo bombers, dive bombers, and fighters. That group attacks the Bremerton Naval shipyard, with devastating results.

A burst of machine-gun fire, followed by a nearby explosion interrupts the officers discussions.

"What the hell is going on out there?"

The yard Commander looks out his corner windows and sees many Japanese planes ravaging the Yard and the ships around it. He returned to his desk, and shouted into the phone, "The Japs are bombing us here!"

The second group attacks the Boeing factory and airport flight line, using fighters and dive bombers. When they return toward the West, every plane on the flight line, including sixth-three new B-17s are flaming wrecks. The cratered Boeing factory buildings are burning.

December 11, 1941, 1300:

President Roosevelt is in a meeting with General Marshal and Admiral King when an aide intrudes with a message for Admiral King.

King gasps, and says, "This can't be true! Get me a conformation!"

"What's happened!" Demanded General Marshal.

King replied, "This message says that the Puget Sound Navy Yard is under attack."

After The Days Of Infamy

Roosevelt said nothing, but his face turned ashen.

December 11, 1941, 1430:

The Strike Force returns, and concentrates their attacks on the Seattle waterfront and industrial centers. The results are even better than expected, with many sinking ships, the waterfront ablaze, and factories destroyed.

December 11, 1941, 1820:

When the last of the Strike Force are recovered, the airship carriers turn Southwest, headed to intercept the two support ships, which have been steaming South at flank speed.

December 12, 1941

Japanese forces land on the southern Philippine Islands of Samar, Jolo, Mindanao.

News of the attack in Washington state astounds the War Department, who have been insisting that the attack at Pearl Harbor was made by most of the Japanese carrier fleet. That a similar sized force hit the Northwest 2800 miles away, only four days later, make it clear that Japan has a much larger carrier fleet than predicted.

The nation's news outlets are on the edge of panic, and Roosevelt's critics demand that those responsible be sacked.

December 12, 1941, 1135:

After the airship carriers resupply, they turn South, and the support ships start their long return to Japan.

A.G. Kimbrough

December 12, 1941, 1300:

The attacking force of 320 planes pass over the Golden Gate Bridge and strike the Bay Area shipyards, the Naval Base at Treasure Island, Mare Island Naval Shipyard, Alameda Naval Air Station, large factories, and ships.

There are no US Carriers in the Bay, but the attack destroyed a dozen seaplanes and several fighters at the air station. Several fighters took off from the air station, and four Japanese dive bombers, three torpedo bombers, and two Zeros are shot down.

December 12, 1941, 1610:

The last planes are recovered and the Airship Carriers head South for a planned launch point fifty miles off the coast of Santa Barbara.

December 13, 1941

The Japanese, under General Yamashita continue their push into Malaya. Under General Homma, the Japanese forces are firmly established in the Northern Philippines, and Hong Kong is threatened.

December 13, 1941, 0630:

The Attack Force of 311 planes cross the coast ten miles south of Santa Barbara, headed East. Twenty minutes later, they turn South.

December 13, 1941, 0715:

The Attack Force hits the Lockheed Factory and airfield in Burbank in a single devastating pass.

The Northrup and North American Aviation aircraft

factories and the Los Angeles Airport receive the same treatment.

December 13, 1941, 0800:

The air raid sirens from LA are heard in Long Beach, and the defenders are getting ready when the attackers appear. A Destroyer cuts the cable to its anchor buoy, and races out of the harbor with General Quarters set. It will be the only warship to survive the attack without damage.

There are 78 AA guns scattered around the area, and they put up a wall of flack that proves to be ineffective.

The torpedo bombers, unused to this point, concentrate on the warships and tankers in the harbor, while the dive bombers use their remaining payloads to hit the Douglas factory.

With no opposition in sight, the fighters strafe the aircraft lined up on the flight line.

After their munitions are spent, the attacking force returns to the airship carriers to re-fuel and re-arm. A dive bomber and two torpedo bombers are lost to AA fire over the harbor. Seventeen ships are damaged or sunk, including a precious oil tanker. The aircraft factories are in flames, and many brand new aircraft are destroyed on the flight line.

December 13, 1941, 1520

San Diego is on alert by the time the Japanese attacking force appears. The 308 planes of the attacking force come out of the sun, led by 97 fighters. Defenders total 84 planes that include a mix of elderly Buffalos, Aircobras, Wildcats, and P-40s.

Fighters engage over North Island, and the Zeros quickly assert their superiority, downing 63 US fighters, while loosing only 24 Zeros.

A flight of US torpedo and dive bombers head Northwest to avoid the fighter battle, in a fruitless attempt to find and destroy the enemy carriers.

The Japanese torpedo and dive bombers vector Southeast to avoid the fighter battle. They then turn North and attack the ships in the San Diego harbor, the shipyard, North Island Naval Air Station, the Ryan Aeronautical Corporation factory, and the completed planes on the flight line.

Between the heavy AA fire and the fighters, the Strike Force torpedo bombers lost 38 planes, and the dive bombers lost 42 planes.

The Japanese aircrews all made an oath to never allow themselves to become captured or reveal the existence of the airship carriers. With 104 planes lost, there were no survivors, and several bodies are recovered with self-inflected bullet wounds.

The damage inflected included several ships sinking, grounded, and damaged. The Ryan factory and North Island's buildings are burning. Over a 60 aircraft are destroyed on the ground.

December 13, 1941, 1745:

Captain Minoru Genda watched as the last aircraft is recovered. His carriers turned West and head for home. They would stop to refuel, 1000 miles East of the home islands, before making the final leg of their long journey.

His forces had accomplished the unthinkable in only seven days. They had destroyed seventy percent of the US

After The Days Of Infamy

Naval forces in the Pacific and wrecked the West Coast aircraft factories and shipyards. He knew the US could recover, but it would take time, and his airship carriers could strike them again and again.

The three or four US carriers still in the Pacific were still a problem, but he had no doubt he would soon vanquish them.

December 14, 1941

In a speech before congress and the country, via radio, Roosevelt attempted to control the panic resulting from the Japanese attacks.

He promised to rebuild the Pacific Fleet by accelerating new construction and transferring ships from the East Coast and reserve fleets to the West Coast.

The coastal air defenses will be expanded to form a Steel Wall against another attack. He also promised to replace the aircraft construction factories with new facilities inland from the West Coast and reported that Boeing just announced that they would expand their factory in Kansas to accommodate the equipment and workers from the damaged Seattle facilities.

Roosevelt had no illusions about the struggle ahead. The country is panicked, and mere words are not enough.

He issued a proclamation establishing Martial Law to quell some areas where riots are threatening, an expanded draft, wage and price controls, and travel limitations.

December 16, 1941

The German offensive around Moscow is now at a complete halt.

Rail traffic in the US is focused on bringing defensive supplies and materials to the West Coast. The transfers include ninety percent of the antiaircraft guns and all the operational fighter and bombing squadrons on the East Coast.

A crash effort produces air search radar sets for the remaining Navy fleet, and the ninety-seven World War One four stack destroyers in the reserve fleet. They are being quickly returned to service and manned by called up, middle aged, World War One veterans, and new recruits fresh out of a rushed two week boot-camp. The new air search radar sets are fitted to these ships, and they are dispatched to the West Coast. They will be stationed 100 miles off the West Coast, to form an early warning picket line. This warning will alert the greatly expanded defensive forces.

December 18, 1941

Japanese troops land on Hong Kong Island.

December 23,1941

A second Japanese landing attempt on Wake Island is successful, and the American garrison surrenders after hours of fighting.

General MacArthur declares Manila an "Open City."

Japanese forces land on Sarawak, Borneo.

December 24, 1941

In the Philippines, American forces retreat into the Bataan Peninsula.

The Japanese bomb Rangoon.

After The Days Of Infamy

December 25, 1941

Hong Kong surrenders to Japan.

December 28, 1941

Japanese paratroopers land on Sumatra.

January 2, 1942

Japanese forces capture Manila. They also take Cavite naval base, and the American and Filipino troops continue their retreat into Bataan.

January 5, 1942

A major Red Army offensive begins, under the command of General Zhukov.

January 7, 1942

The Soviet Winter counter-offensive comes to a halt, after a Zeppelin Aircraft Carrier based attack on the headquarters of General Zhukov. All four carriers were refitted to carry a dozen Stuka dive bombers. The carriers made a run from Germany to the front where the low cloud deck had grounded most aircraft. The Stuka strike force are able to home on to the radio transmissions coming from Zhukov's headquarters. They dropped below the cloud deck to make attack runs at less than 100 feet. Although a third of the Stukas are lost to ground fire, the balance of the force are able to locate and return to their carriers flying above the clouds and transmitting homing signals.

Unlike most of his staff, Zhukov is not killed, but his injuries will keep him out of action for months.

The combination of the reinforcements brought to the front after the British surrender, and the decapitation of Zhukov and his staff, forces Stalin to realize that Moscow may fall in the spring.

'Operation Barbarossa' has been renewed.

The siege of the Bataan Peninsula begins.

January 11, 1942

Japanese troops capture Kuala Lumpur, Malaya.

Japan invades the Dutch East Indies.

January 15, 1942

Lt. Wycliff is promoted to Lt. Commander. He is now in command of a Blimp squadron that is being transferred to a new base in Panama City, Panama. Their mission is to provide anti-sub patrols for the Westbound convoys leaving the Canal.

He finds the ladies in Panama City lovely, and frequently willing to have brief affairs with American Officers.

January 19, 1942

Japanese forces take large numbers of British troops prisoner, North of Singapore.

After The Days Of Infamy

January 22, 1942

USS Fletcher, DD 445, the first of a next generation destroyer class, is placed in commission. Originally scheduled for commissioning in June of 42, but a top priority crash effort pushed it forward, because Halsey desperately needs its radar and upgraded anti-air defense firepower capabilities.

January 25, 1942

Japanese troops invade the Solomon Islands.

January 28, 1942

The Enterprise Task Force meets a convoy leaving the Panama Canal and escorts them toward Pearl Harbor.

The convoy includes six radar equipped World War One, four stack destroyers from the reserve fleet, five loaded tankers, a sub-tender, eight loaded freighters, and the twelve fleet submarines, in commission, that were on the East Coast.

January 30, 1942

USS Fletcher begins a flank run down the East Coast to the Panama Canal with a full wartime load of food, fuel, and ammunition.

January 31, 1942

The Japanese take the port of Moulamein, Burma; they now threaten Rangoon as well as Singapore.

On the Eastern front, the Russians are in retreat at several points.

A.G. Kimbrough

February 11, 1942

The two airship support ships depart Japan, one, headed for a point 2000 miles West of the Panama Canal, and the other, for the South Pacific.

February 15, 1942

Enterprise leads the convoy into Pearl Harbor. After refueling, the Enterprise Task Force departs to an area 200 miles North of Hawaii. They will provide an early warning of a Japanese carrier group returning.

Two of the freighters are full of crated P-40s, their pilots, and support crews. Two of the other freighters carry construction equipment and supplies for a Sea Bee battalion. The Sea Bees will start to repair airstrips and fuel storage areas. The balance of the freighters are carrying food, ammunition and supplies for the island forces. When Wheeler field, and the P-40s are operational, a flight of B-17s will arrive, and the Enterprise Task Force can be relieved from providing the island air cover.

As soon as the subs are refueled and provisioned with fresh food, they scatter to start an unrelenting submarine war against Japanese shipping.

March 11, 1942

Airship Task Group I (ASC1, Mount Fugi and ASC2, Kaga), depart Japan, headed for the Panama Canal. Their orders call for repetitive attacks on the canal locks until they are all destroyed.

Airship Task Group II (ASC3, Soryu, and ASC4, Hiryu) leave Japan bound for the South Pacific. Captain Minoru Genda is not pleased at splitting his carrier forces, but he understands the need for him to be where he will most likely encounter the American carriers in the South Pacific.

March 12, 1942

The Fletcher exits the Panama Canal and heads West toward a location 1000 miles south of Hawaii where they will join the Enterprise and the rest of her Task Force.

March 14, 1942

Mt Fugi is 2000 miles West of Panama, and will attack the Canal the following afternoon. The Kaga is running fifty miles to the North, headed for the same objective.

Captain Torinaga orders his crew to get a good nights sleep since the next day will have lots of action. The airships move through the night at ninety-three knots, with a minimal crew manning the Airship's stations.

March 15, 1942, 0300:

Fletcher is running at twenty-six knots on a Southwest heading. The ship is at Condition Three, where a third of the crew is at battle stations, and all watertight hatches are shut. Both the sonar and the Radars are operating in active search modes.

0315:

Lt. Jg. Elmer Price, the Mustang Gunnery Officer is in the Mk 37 director, when a report from the Fire Control Radar operator comes through his sound powered phones.

"Damn it!, Either this radar is crapped out, or there's a monster object at 035 degrees, 25,000 yards, headed this way at over fifty knots."

Within seconds, the alarm rang out, "General Quarters,

General Quarters, All Hands Man Your Battle Stations, Air Action Starboard!"

The Captain, Lt. Cmdr. William M. Cole, reached the bridge in less than thirty seconds, and quickly decided to break radio silence and call Halsey.

0320:

Halsey's reply left no doubt, "It's not ours. Engage when in range. We are launching an all fighter air strike. It should reach your location about sunrise."

Captain Cole came back on the sound-powered phone circuit, and said, "When the range gets down to 17,000 yards, let me know. We'll turn to 0280 to let all guns bear. Commence Firing when all guns are clear to fire."

The Fletcher had been equipped with two hundred rounds of the still experimental proximity shells, and half of them had been distributed to the ready service magazines. Price ordered the guns loaded with those shells.

0326:

Mount 55, the gun nearest the stern, cleared the superstructure, and Price ordered, "Commence Firing."

He watched, with his binoculars as the five-inch shells reached into the darkness. Over half of the five gun salvo exploded near the target, briefly illuminating it. It was an airship, larger than anything he had ever seen.

The second salvo was in the air before the first exploded. Two shells from first exploded below the cabin at the bottom of the craft. A fire broke out, and subsequent shells kept exploding ahead and below the airship. Several small fires burn at the cabin base, and on the sides of the airship.

Price exclaimed, "We're not doing enough damage!" He then ordered, "Switch to Standard HE shells, with fuses set to predicted target range."

The next salvo fired, and Price could see the internal explosions through the Airship's skin. An internal fire blazed up and then died back down after the third salvo.

0328:

When the next salvo exploded, there were a massive series of secondary explosions that tore the airship apart. The flaming debris fragments rained down on the ocean for the next ten minutes.

After a cease fire announcement, the topside crew of the Fletcher, watched as the Destroyer approached the still expanding debris field. The ship slowed, and then stopped just in front of a patch of ocean littered with pieces of the airship, aircraft, and body parts.

Price's reflection is interrupted by the radar operator.

"There's another Airship to the North, headed away from us."

Within another minute, the Fletcher was turning to starboard, and approaching flank speed. The Enterprise fighters were on a new vector, and the Fletcher was racing to keep the new target in radar range.

0545:

The Eastern horizon was shifting from grey to gold when the radar operator reported planes launching from the airship.

Two planes were spotted heading in their direction and soon identified as Zeros. Price requested the bridge lookouts to keep tracking the airship and ordered the radar to track the closest plane, and all guns should engage them when they came into range.

0553:

The lead Zero had avoided the five-inch bursts, and started a strafing run, but is obliterated by fire from one of the twin 40 millimeter guns.

0610:

More planes left the airship, and head toward the Fletcher. The planes proved to be Stuka dive bombers, supported by more Zeros. For the next ten minutes the Fletcher remained under constant attack, twisting and turning, her guns keeping a wall of steel between her and the attackers. The proximity shells were working well on the Stukas. Fletcher took three close hits and is strafed twice.

The airship was moving to the edge of visual range, and another flight of Stukas was approaching. The damage control parties are desperately working to control the flooding caused by the near misses, and the corpsmen were tending to the wounded, while the airship launched more planes.

0620:

Again, the walls of steel knocked out most of the first wave. But, two Stukas get through the defensive fire. The first, was hit, and the bomb exploded 50 yards to Port.

When the second Stuka was hit, it plunged into the top of Mount 53, and exploded. Fortunately, the torpedo tubes just forward of Mount 53, did not explode. However, the blast and fire knocked out Mounts 53 and 54, the After Steering Station, the Twin 40 mm mount above it, and all six of the 20 mm mounts around it. Mount 55 was still operational under manual control.

0630:

The Fletcher continued running at flank speed as another wave of attackers approached. Fortunately, the lead flight of Hellcats were able to intercept the approaching Stukas, and knocked them all out of the sky. Captain Cole ordered the ships speed cut to one third, until the damage control parties could bring the topside fires control.

0635:

The second flight of Hellcats quickly disposed of the two Zeros that had just launched. They also caught two more on the elevator just before they could launch, and left them and the flight deck in a flaming ruin. The Hellcats exhausted their ammunition in a futile attempt to deliver a knock-out blow to the airship.

0640:

The Lead Hellcat flight reached the Airship, and Lt. Michael Boyd ordered his flight to use their remaining ammunition to knock out the Airships engines. The engines were located in pods around the middle of the airship. After Lt. Boyd knocked out the final pod with his last 20 rounds, he sent a message over the TBS to the Fletcher, "We've done all we can, you will have to finish this job. The airship is directly Northeast of you, without power, and burning."

The Fletcher's reply was brief, "Will do."

It took an hour to bring the fires on the Fletcher under control.

Although the lookouts lost sight of the Airship, the radar was able to lock on, shortly after the Fletcher came back to flank speed. In a discussion with Captain Cole, Price confirmed they could easily kill the airship as soon as they were in range, but he suggested they should get as much film on it before they did.

0815:

When the airship came in sight, fires burned on two engine pods, and the flight deck. The airship was at 6,000 feet, without forward motion, and slowly sinking. The Fletcher approached to within 2,000 yards of the airship and used up all the film on the ship.

In a series of radio messages with Halsey, he directed Captain Cole to stand by, and attempt to capture the hulk if possible. The Task Force would arrive before dark.

0945:

The airship had sunk to 5,000 feet, and it must have been obvious that the Fletcher was just waiting to capture it when it settled to the ocean.

0952:

Price was watching with binoculars, when to his horror, he saw hatches and windows opening, and people plunging through them.

The exodus of the airship continued for a couple of minutes before the airship exploded. Many crewmen jumped to their deaths, preferring that quick end to burning as the flaming wreckage settled to the ocean surface.

1720:

After The Days Of Infamy

When the Enterprise Task Force arrived to find only a section of the airship tail still floating on the surface. Fletcher came alongside the Enterprise and transferred the most seriously wounded. Fletcher's Exec had been at the After Control Station, and was killed, along with 63 others.

Halsey requested Captain Cole to come aboard, for an after action conference. Cole took Lt. Jg. Price with him, since he had directed the gunnery action throughout the entire battle. It was after midnight before they returned to the Fletcher.

March 16, 1942 0900:

In an exchange over TBS, Captain Cole insisted he could not leave his wounded ship to fly back to Washington, and debrief a bunch of paper-pushers. Finally Halsey relented and agreed to send the Mustang Gunnery Officer in his place. Lt. Jg., Price impressed Halsey, the night before, and he did not want to replace Cole with someone who didn't know this new class DD. If his Exec had not been killed, he might have insisted, but he needed the Fletcher in his Task force.

1300:

Lt. Jg. Price joined Lt. Boyd, the fighter squadron leader, board a seaplane that flew to the Enterprise Task Force location from Panama. The ocean chop was moderate, so just before the seaplane arrived, Enterprise pumped out several hundred gallons of fuel oil to reduce it.

Lt. Boyd is pissed, because he killed two Stukas, and only needed one more kill to become an ace. Lt. Jg. Price is pleased at the prospect of going to DC, because his wife and kids were in Northern Virginia, and he hadn't seen them since last August.

There was a B17 waiting for them at Panama City, and they left within two hours after the seaplane landed. They found the B17 no more comfortable for passengers than the seaplane.

March 17, 1942

U.S. General Douglas MacArthur arrived in Australia, after leaving his headquarters in the Philippines, under a direct order from the President.

March 18, 1942

1500 miles Northeast of Hawaii: After receiving only one garbled message from the Kaga, the Task Force I support ship turned toward home, broke radio silence, and transmitted, "Lost contact with Task Force I. Received a partial message from the Kaga on March fifteenth, that stated they were under attack by fighter aircraft, send help."

"We are returning to base."

March 18, 1942 0900:

After only six hours sleep, and in traveled, rumpled uniforms, Lt. Boyd and Lt. Jg. Price arrived at the main conference room at the Navy Department. There were four Admirals, including the CNO, already at the table, plus several civilians. One wall is plastered with blow-up pictures from the film the two hand carried to Washington.

The conference went on for two days before breaking into smaller groups. Lt. Boyd was with a group from NAVAIR, and Lt. Jg. Price with one from NAVORD.

After The Days Of Infamy

March 19, 1942, 1045:

Rio and Mickey were in a Tokyo meeting devoted to resource planning when an aide came in and called Mickey away for an urgent telephone call. When he returned to the meeting, as it was ending, his face was grave. He suggested that Rio join him at his office for some tea.

When his office door closed, Mickey said, "Task Group I is gone. All we know is the Kaga reported a fighter attack, and then nothing more. I'm afraid that the damned Americans have found a way to kill the airships."

Rio replied, "I don't understand how they could have even been discovered. The doctrine required them to be moving at over ninety miles per hour and separated by over fifty miles. I also can't believe fighters could have brought them down. The tests you ran on the prototype nose section showed little damage from even fifty caliber tracers, even when they punctured gasoline tanks and started fires. The Helium leaking from holes in the bladder quickly extinguished the fire. Even a five-inch shell didn't damage the bamboo structure, and it went all the way through without detonating the impact fuse."

Mickey sighed, and said, "I remember those tests, and just don't understand. Everyone is in a panic. Yamamoto even suggested withdrawing Task Group II until we can find out what happened."

March 20, 1942

Heinrich visited Maria several times after Rolf was killed. She now found the work on war wounded to be increasingly depressing. He gave her a job at the Zeppelin Works as a staff nurse. They had been dating over the last year, and Heinrich was falling in love. They had kissed passionately, but he was always careful to not push it any further. This day, he prepared a dinner at his apartment. After the coffee is served, he asked her to marry him.

She broke into tears, and then said, "I love you, and I'm more than willing to be your lover and mistress. But, I can't marry you because my Grandmother is Jewish. The Nazi persecution of Jews gets worse every day, and I can't let my love put you at risk."

Heinrich embraced her, and spent the evening, and the night in an attempt to convince her he could protect her. His position and wealth made him immune to any threats from the Jew haters. He promised to take her away if a threat should materialize. She finally agreed, and they were married in a Lutheran ceremony the following week.

March 24, 1942

The USS Sculpin SS191, was on patrol in the Banda Sea. She spotted a large, fast moving convoy, but the sub was not in a position to catch up to it. Just before midnight, she encountered a freighter, with an odd very tall mast structure on the bow. It was lagging behind the convoy, and the sub fired a spread of three torpedoes at near maximum range. They heard one explosion before loosing contact with the freighter.

March 25, 1942

With the looming surrender of the last American forces in the Philippines, Roosevelt is desperate to shore up the Public Opinion. Against the advice of the Chief of Naval Operations, he issues this statement:

"A few days ago, in the Pacific, off the coast of Panama, US Naval Forces under the command of Admiral Halsey intercepted, and destroyed, two Japanese aircraft carriers.

"These were not conventional aircraft carrier ships, but rather huge Zeppelins. The mystery of the almost simultaneous attacks at Pearl Harbor, and the West Coast has been solved. These airships were tracked moving at nearly 100 miles per hour. These two airship carriers were likely the same force that carried out the earlier attacks on Pearl Harbor and the West Coast.

"The defensive steps we have taken have proven to be effective in counteracting this threat. While this threat remains, we are improving our defenses against it every day.

"One last item to report, is the success of our submarine forces, who are drawing a tightening noose around the Japanese naval forces operating in the South Pacific, and beyond."

The statement is released with two photographs. The first photograph is from a fighter's gun camera, and showed the second airship carrier, with two of its engine pods blazing.

Taken through a US submarine's periscope, the second photograph showed a large freighter, it's keel broken in two and sinking.

March 25. 1942, 1100

When the support ship for Airship Task Group II broke radio silence, reporting it had been hit with a torpedo, and was sinking. Both ASC3, Soryu, and ASC4, Hiryu heard the message, and diverted to the newly captured island of Rabaul, where an air base is under construction.

A.G. Kimbrough

March 26, 1942

Rio received a call from Mickey, who asked him over for tea. Again, after the office door closed, Mickey reported that the Task Group II support ship was torpedoed, and both Soryu, and Hiryu have landed on Rabaul Island at an airbase that is under construction.

Rio looked surprised, and said, "They have no support on the island, and they can't operate out of there."

Mickey shook his head, and said, "I know. And with the increasing number of freighter losses, I doubt the airship support ship from Task Group I could even reach there without a heavy escort, and it would take three weeks to reach Rabaul, if they are zigzagging. That's why I recommended to Yamamoto that we bring them both home. He has not released the orders for their return yet, but he released production orders on the next two airships."

Rio injected, "Its good they don't use much aluminum. You know how short the supply is getting now."

March 27, 1942

Lt. Jg. Price was looking forward to spending the weekend with his family, before he returned to the Fletcher. He had until Monday morning before he had to return to NAVORD. He walked into the room he shared with Lt. Boyd at the BOQ and found him packing.

Lt. Boyd was ecstatic, after receiving orders to rejoin Halsey, just before a new and important offensive operation. He would fly to San Francisco where he would catch the Hornet when she sailed to join the Enterprise.

After The Days Of Infamy

March 29, 1942

Rio was enjoying his second pot of tea when Mickey's call came in. "Can you meet me for a working lunch in my office? I need to discuss the Helium delivery schedules for the rest of the year."

Rio knew Helium deliveries were not the subject Mickey wanted to discuss.

Mickey was looking worried. He said, "The news came in from the Spanish Embassy this morning. The Americans admitted shooting down the Mount Fugi and Kaga."

Rio gasped, and questioned, "What is the War Department reaction?"

Mickey replied, "They're in a panic. Yamamoto ordered the immediate return of Task Force Two. The Army is raising hell, blaming the Navy for the delays in the South Pacific campaign."

March 30, 1942

When Lt. Jg. Price reported to NAVORD on Monday morning, he is directed to report to a different office in another one of the World War One vintage buildings. He is surprised to be meeting with the Director of the Office of Naval Intelligence. Price recognized him from some earlier high-level meetings.

The Director offered and poured him a cup of coffee before speaking. "I suppose you are curious about why you haven't yet received orders to return to the Fletcher."

"I've assumed that someone still needed me to answer more questions."

The Director smiled and said, "Well, Mr. Price, I need you here with me, working on deciding how best to deal

A.G. Kimbrough

with the airship threats. Since you're the only man in the Navy to have killed one, your inputs are essential. We know your family is in Fairfax, and this assignment will usually let you see them on weekends. Hopefully, you agree because you don't really have a choice. Because you will lose sea pay, I'll try to make it up to you, and this set of new railroad tracks should help."

The Director handed him a set of Lt. Bars, and said, "Your new office is across the hall. I want you to start work on a report, identifying actions we can take that will neutralize the airship threats."

Elmer went home instead of the BOQ that night, and took his wife, Helen, out to dinner to celebrate his promotion and the new assignment. Helen had accepted his Naval career and the risks he might face in wartime. But, she was thrilled that he would not return to the war soon. The promotion was nice, but they didn't need the money, since she had more than enough.

The drive back to their country home became a sexually charged event, with Helen's actions making Elmer have difficulty keeping his eyes on the road. When they arrived back at home, Helen insisted that Elmer make love to her in the moonlight, on the balcony off their bedroom. She had a strong sex drive that matched his own. They had both agreed that in times of separation, monogamy would not be a necessity, if the transgressions were kept discrete.

March 30, 1942

The Callahans usually took the bus once a month to spend a couple of days enjoying the city and shopping for things not available in their village. They had an appointment with a Doctor to confirm that Hekoi was pregnant. Wade ran the batteries down on their Attwater-

Kent short wave radio, while listening to the war news. A new battery pack was on their purchase list. Wade was anxious for a news update, because the battery finally expired two weeks before then.

The couple arrived late in the afternoon, and Hekoi was tired. They checked into a nice hotel and enjoyed a room service dinner before retiring. Wade woke early and left a note for the still sleeping Hekoi.

He went downstairs, purchased a couple of papers, and was enjoying a cup of coffee, while reading the most recent Newspapers. Wade finished the English version of the Havana daily paper and unfolded the Miami Herald.

He abruptly stood, overturning his coffee, when the pictures, and the headline sunk in. "US Navy Kills a Pair of Jap Zeppelin Carriers."

After reading the complete story, including Roosevelt's statement, He exclaimed, "Oh my God, now it all makes sense."

Wade raced back to their room and found Hekoi just getting out of bed. He kissed her, and said, "Good morning love, we have a lot to talk about. Do you want me to have room service bring up some breakfast for you?"

She smiled and replied, "just some tea, please. What made you so energized today?"

"I just put it together, the Japanese Navy has airship carriers that they used to attack Pearl Harbor and the West Coast. I knew the Germans couldn't be using all the Helium we were shipping. I have to go to Washington. Do you want to stay here, or go back to the village? I'm sure I can hire a midwife to stay with you while I'm gone."

Hekoi frowned, and said, "Mr. Callahan, I wouldn't stay

in Japan, even if it meant sailing half way around the world with you. I won't let you leave me in Cuba, while you go running off to Washington, for who knows how long."

Wade interrupted, "But in your condition it might be dangerous to travel, and we can't just take a boat to Miami, because the Japanese could have people watching the port. Plus, the government's putting Japanese people in internment camps."

Tears streamed down her cheeks, and she said, "If this is something you have to do, I'm sure you are clever enough to figure out how to make it happen. I know pregnant women travel all the time, and the doctor will confirm it for you."

That afternoon, Wade visited the Barclay's Bank branch and withdrew $10,000 in cash. Hekoi's doctor confirmed that she was in fine shape, despite being pregnant. He told the couple she would be in no danger from traveling. That evening Wade tracked down a local printer who forged Passports on the side. He took Hekoi's picture and promised to have her Cuban Passport ready the next afternoon.

The next morning, Wade visited Havana's largest Yacht Broker, and directed him to find an ocean going motor-sailor with fuel capacity to reach Washington DC without having to refuel.

During the afternoon, the couple picked up Hekoi's passport and shopped for supplies for their voyage.

March 31, 1942

After spending the day evaluating three different boats, Wade purchased a five-year-old, thirty-seven-foot boat, built by the same British shipyard as the Sunflower. The

Blueberry had been ordered by a man who lost everything when the market crashed.

The next owner bought it at a discount and had it delivered to his home in Baltimore. He sailed it around the Chesapeake Bay until last year. Then he had the boat overhauled, in anticipation of making an around the world cruise. His around the world voyage made it as far as Havana before he had a fatal heart attack. His wife just wanted to get the money out and sold it to Wade for $9,000.

The next morning the couple sailed Blueberry up the coast to the village where they had lived since leaving the liner.

When they finished loading and disposing of their things, the Blueberry set sail for Washington DC.

April 2, 1942

Hornet and Task Force 18 got underway from San Francisco Bay at 0848 with the 16 B-25 bombers in clear view on the flight deck.

April 7, 1942

In a DC meeting between Henry J. Kaiser and Howard Hughes, They dissolved their partnership to develop the HK-1 flying boat heavy lift transport. It was now obvious to both men that the Army Air Corps would not be issuing a contract for the prototype. Hughes is still intrigued by the prospect of using wood structures for large aircraft airframes, but his ideas had no salable applications in sight.

A.G. Kimbrough

April 13, 1942

The Blueberry docked in a long-term slip at the Potomac Yard Yacht Club, just before dusk. The next morning Wade took a cab over to DC. He knew a Congressman, who had been a friend of his father. It took three calls from the Willard Hotel's lobby to reach Congressman Warren Moore, who remembered their only meeting.

Wade told the Congressman that he recently escaped from Japan where he had been working since 1929. Wade said he had information about the Airship Carriers, he was sure the Navy would want to know. But, he didn't know who to contact. The Congressman told him he would find out, and for Wade to call him at 9:00 AM the next day.

Wade took a cab back to the Yacht Club, with a stop in route, to pick up Chinese food for their dinners. Hekoi was nervous by the time Wade returned and pleased at having dinner she didn't have to cook. They went to bed early and made love for the first time since leaving Cuba.

Wade returned to the Willard the next morning and called the Congressman at 9:00 AM. The Congressman told him that a Navy vehicle would be outside the hotel at 10:30, and it would take him over for a meeting with the Director of Naval Intelligence. The Congressman said he had to hang up, but to be sure to come see him.

As he walked out of the hotel, Wade realized that he didn't know the Director's name. The sailor behind the jeep's wheel only knew the office location.

A Civilian at the front desk proved to be rude, and not interested in Wade's request to see the Director. When the man demanded all the details about Wade's information, Wade said he doubted if the man had a high enough clearance for them. That reply started the man yelling for the Marine guard outside the office.

As the Marine was about to escort Wade out, a Navy Lt. came through the inner office door. Lt. Price had just finished a meeting with his boss, and he asked Wade what the problem was.

Wade explained that he escaped from Japan just before Pearl Harbor, and had some critical intelligence for the Director, but the guy at the desk would not let him go in to see the him.

Price told the Marine he could return to his post and then took Wade by the arm and led him into the Director's office. He introduced Wade to Director Roger Kelly, a retired Navy Captain. Director Kelly remembered the call from Congressman Moore, and was expecting to spend an hour with Mr. Callahan, listening to what he had to say, as a courtesy to the Congressman. He was not expecting to learn much of anything useful.

By lunchtime, the Director's assessment of what Wade had to say, had changed. He asked, "Lt. Price, can you take Wade over to the cafeteria, I have to shuffle my schedule. This will probably take the rest of today, and tomorrow. Please bring me back a glass of tea and a ham sandwich."

When the door closed, Director Kelly picked up the phone, and called J. Edgar Hoover. He asked him to do a complete, Top Secret background check on Wade Callahan. He also asked to have an agent at the Willard Hotel lobby at 5:30 PM, to follow Callahan when the Navy driver dropped him off at the door.

When the meeting resumed, Wade started relating everything he knew about the Helium wells and processing plant, including pinpointing their exact locations.

The meeting broke up at 1730, and the Navy driver dropped him off at the Willard.

As the FBI agent watched, Wade walked into the lobby, briefly wait, and then walked back out to the cab stand. Then the FBI agent had to run back to his car, as the cab Wade took pulled away from the curb. It was necessary for the agent to run a light to keep Wade's cab in sight. By then, it was almost two blocks ahead of him.

Traffic was heavy, and the Agent lost the cab on the Fourteenth Street Bridge. A car between him and the cab rear-ended another cab, and traffic stopped. After crossing the bridge, Wade had the cab stop at another Chinese restaurant, where he purchased a takeout dinner.

Hekoi was pleased to have Wade return with supper and a bottle of sake. Worried, and bored during the day, she stayed out of sight below deck. During dinner, Wade said he would insist on protection for her at the start of the morning meeting. If the government would not give that guarantee, then they would sail back to Cuba.

April 14, 1942

Director Kelly was reading the FBI report when the intercom buzzed. His gatekeeper, asked if he was ready to see Mr. Callahan.

Kelly replied, "Take him over to Price's office, I'll call when I'm ready to see them, and get them some coffee and sweet rolls."

The FBI report was brief. Callahan was born in Waco, Texas, and had taken a drilling rig to Japan in 1929. He had a six figure account at Barclay's Bank, and there was a record of his return to Hawaii on a disabled motor sailor on June 16, 1940. There was an international warrant from the

After The Days Of Infamy

Japanese government for his arrest on charges of the theft of the motor sailor Sunflower, and the murder of its owner, Rionitsi (Rio) Watnabe.

The State Department released him after he produced a bill of sale for the Sunflower, and a letter from its owner, and a Mr. Mitsumi (Mickey) Imazumi that stated they helped Mr. Callahan and his wife escape from a "witch hunt" by the government secret police.

On June 20, 1940, Callahan and his wife departed Hawaii for Miami on a passenger liner. They were not on the liner when it arrived in Miami. Their luggage was still in their cabin, along with a suicide note that said the couple were afraid that Japanese agents would be waiting for them in Miami, and couldn't stand the thought of being always on the run from them. They planned to jump overboard during the night cruise to Mami. The Purser said his records showed the couple disembarked in Havana and returned to the ship two hours later.

When the FBI agent attempted to tail Callahan's cab lost it on the Fourteenth Street Bridge, he could not find out where Callahan was staying.

As the Director was getting ready to call Price and Callahan into his office, the FBI called his direct line. This morning, the agent had interviewed the driver of the cab Callahan took to the Willard. That cab driver reported picking Callahan up at the Potomac Yard Yacht Club, and the agent was prepared to go there and determine where Callahan was staying.

Kelly told the agent to go there, but stay in the marina office until he received further instructions.

Wade and Elmer Price were the same age, and had quickly become friends, by the time of the call from the

Director. They walked into the conference room and sat down at the table. Director Kelly was sitting at the head and held a file.

He smiled and said, "Good morning gentlemen."

After Price had replied, Wade said, "Good morning, sir. Before we get started, I have a request that I consider urgent. My pregnant wife, Hekoi, was born in Japan, and I will not tolerate the possibility of her being placed in a detention camp.

"Because I'm a patriot, I traveled here from Cuba to provide my country information I consider vital to our war effort. However, I must have a guarantee that she will be immune from any action by the government, because she is Japanese. Knowing feelings against the Japanese are high here in America, I'm prepared to protect and provide for her.

No matter what the decision is about providing that immunity, I will spend today giving you all the additional information I can."

"If my government cannot provide that immunity, then we will return to Cuba. I'm willing to provide further support, but it would have to be from there."

Director Kelly's expression gave no clue when he replied, "You know, I can prevent you from leaving, and force your cooperation, because this effort has the highest priority. I believe you understand that."

Wade shrugged, and said, "Yes I do, but I believe you and my government are honorable. Getting Hekoi immunity is the honorable thing to do."

The Director stood, and said, "Let me make a couple of calls to start the immunity process. I'll get it done, even if I have to play hardball with Roosevelt. You may want to review this report with Lt. Price while I'm gone."

Director Kelly's first call was to the FBI agent at the marina. He directed him to maintain surveillance and provide armed protection for Mrs Callahan against any and all threats.

That call is followed by calls to the Secretary of State, Congressman Moore, and the President.

When the Director Kelley returned, he said, "Well I got the ball rolling, and I'm sure we will be successful in getting Hekoi immunity. Roosevelt agrees. All we need to do is get all the right paperwork filled out and signed."

The discussions continued all day, and Wade provided a profile of both Rio and Mickey. By the end of the next day, he is offered a job as a civilian employee of the Navy to work with Lt. Price on the Director's staff, for the duration.

Hekoi was thrilled when the immunity paperwork is signed, and the couple spent the weekend as guests of Elmer Price and his wife Helen at their horse farm in Fairfax, Virginia. The ladies become fast friends during the weekend. On Sunday night after dinner, the couples enjoyed a soak in the tub beside the indoor pool. Helen was uncertain about suggesting they soak in the nude, but Hekoi said it was how they soaked at home. Then she proudly showed off her beginning baby bump.

During the soak, Helen offered to rent the Callahans a cottage on the grounds. The guys could commute to DC together, and both ladies would enjoy the company. The offer is accepted, and the Callahans move into the cottage on the following weekend. They find it was a nice change from the cramped quarters on the Bluebell. They continue to enjoy dinner and soaks with Elmer and Helen, one or two times a week.

April 18, 1942

Rio and Mickey are having an early lunch together before yet another meeting. Rio was looking at a report from the Secret Police that Mickey obtained. It stated that Wade Callahan and his wife escaped Hawaii before the agents there could eliminate them. The Kempeitai had a team of Mafia assassins waiting at the dock in Miami. But, the couple did not get off the ship.

Later, an investigation reviled that the couple committed suicide the evening before the ship reached Miami. The note found in their cabin showed that they could not face the thought of being returned to Japan, or spending the rest of their lives hiding from the Secret Police agents. The Kempeitai now considered the case closed.

Both men agreed that they did not believe the Callahans had committed suicide.

They were just finishing a last cup of tea when the air raid sirens started. Both men ran to the roof and looked across the city. There was smoke rising over the harbor, and they could hear the sounds of anti-aircraft guns, and then, the sound of aircraft engines approaching.

Rio had the best eyesight, and he pointed and said, "Look!"

Approaching them was a single twin-engine aircraft, flying just over the rooftops. Mickey exclaimed, "It's a B-25! That's not a carrier plane."

They watched as the plane flew out of sight toward the West.

With a profound sadness in his voice, Mickey

commented, "The Americans have now attacked the homeland. The dragon has truly been awakened. I fear the future will not be in our favor."

April 22, 1942

In a meeting in Tokyo with Naval, Army, and Government leaders, the decision is made to not return the Airship Force II to the South Pacific. That Force, and the two new Airship Carriers being built, will form a long range defensive perimeter around the home islands. They must prevent another repetition of a raid on the homeland.

<u>The Dragon Wakes</u>

May 3, 1942

In the initial move of the Japanese strategic plan to capture Port Moresby, Japanese forces make unopposed landings on Tuglagi, opening the Battle of the Coral Sea.

American General Stilwell decides that nothing more can be accomplished in Burma, and that the time has come to evacuate.

May 4, 1942

US Rear Admiral Fletcher's Task Force 17 makes the first carrier strike of the Battle of the Coral Sea attacking

Japanese naval targets near Tulagi.

May 6, 1942

On Corregidor, Lt. General Wainwright surrendered the last U.S. forces in the Philippines to Lt. General Homma. About 12,000 are made prisoners. Homma will face criticism from his superiors over the amount of time it has taken him to reduce the Philippines, and be forced into retirement.

May 7, 1942

In the Coral Sea, Japanese search planes from the light carrier Shoho spot and sink the tanker USS Neosho and destroyer USS Sims. Later, planes from USS Lexington and USS Yorktown stumble across light carrier Shoho while pursuing a false report. The US planes sink her, leading to the first use in the American Navy of the signal, "Scratch one flattop." Admiral Inoue is so alarmed by the loss of Shoho, that he halts the Port Moresby invasion group until the American carriers can be found and destroyed.

After riding the Hornet as a spare pilot, Lt. Boyd transfers to the Yorktown to replace a lost Squadron leader. He shoots down two Zeros in the first day of the Battle of the Coral Sea.

May 8, 1942

Each Navy finally locates the other's main carrier groups, and several attacks follow.

Only Zuikaku escapes unscathed;

Shokaku has her flight deck bent, requiring two months repairs;

After The Days Of Infamy

Lexington is sunk and Yorktown damaged.

When both fleets retire Admiral Inoue cancels the Port Moresby operation. This is the first significant failure of a Japanese strategic operation in the Pacific Theater.

The loss of the Shoho and the damage to the Shokaku leave the Auikaku as the only operational Japanese ship carrier in the South Pacific. Admiral Inoue demands the return of at least one Airship Carrier, but that request is rejected. He is directed to accelerate completion of the airfield on Guadalcanal.

The second day, after two more kills, a machine-gun bullet cuts an oil line and the engine sizes as Lt. Boyd attempts to land on the Yorktown. A Destroyer picked him out of the water, with several injuries.

May 13, 1942

Lt. Boyd arrives at the San Diego Naval Hospital, where he is taken to surgery. Later that day, he awakens to see a familiar face. Dorthy Rogers is the widow of Boyd's best friend at the Naval Academy, who was killed at Pearl Harbor. Dorthy went back to school after that day, and now works as a civilian nurse.

Boyd sees her almost every day during his recovery. When Dorthy's best friend dumped Boyd shortly after he went to Flight School, he refused to get serious about anyone. Love em and leave em was his motto, but he was becoming serious about Dorthy. She was also serious about him.

May 30, 1942

With the ship carrier losses and the airship carriers defending the home islands, the planned invasions of

Midway and Alaska are canceled. Those forces are shifted to the South Pacific.

June 9, 1942

In a meeting with the Goodyear-Zeppelin company, Howard Hughes is unsuccessful in setting up a partnership to develop a wood framed Airship Carrier. The well publicized losses of the US Navy's Airships and Goodyear's current backlog of blimp orders made the partnership a bad business decision, despite Howard's enthusiasm.

June 18, 1942

The Manhattan Project is started, and is the beginning of a scientific approach to nuclear weapons.

July 3,1942

Guadalcanal is now firmly in the hands of the Japanese.

July 10, 1942

With the looming threat of more airship carrier attacks, the team at the Office of Naval Intelligence focus on reducing the threat. With the known location of the Helium wells and processing plant, they studied ways to attack and destroy them.

Because the Helium gas is lost through venting and leaks, during airship flight operations, it must be replaced. If it is not available, it would have to be replaced with Hydrogen. That replacement would make the airships much more vulnerable to tracers.

Army Air Corps representatives said the B-29 could fly

After The Days Of Infamy

from an Alaska airfield to Hokkaido and back, but the bomb load would be very limited. Because of the attack on the Boeing factory in Seattle, and the loss of both prototype B-29s, everything had been moved to Wichita, Kansas. The new prototypes would not be ready to fly until late in 1942, and no production aircraft would be available until early 1944.

Wade doubted that even several 1000 pound bombs, could damage the wells bad enough to be unrepairable.

After a frustrating morning with no solutions in sight, Wade and Lt. Price went to the cafeteria in the next building, which had a crab cake special that day. The cafeteria was full, and they took the last seats at a small table in a corner, where a Navy Captain was seated. They talked as they ate, and found out that Captain Anderson, a Materials Engineer, had spearheaded development of the ceramic armor for the Iowa.

Wade raised a question about what material would be best to achieve the deepest ground penetration for a 1000 pound bomb. Captain Anderson replied that they should discuss this subject in a classified location.

By the time the afternoon meeting broke up, Captain Anderson had convinced the team that multiple salvos of 2700 pound, 16 inch armor piercing shells with impact delayed fuses, and fired at maximum elevation would offer the best means to make the wells unrecoverable for a very long time. He became the newest member of the Project Javelin team, and soon developed a feasibility test to be performed at the Navy's Dahlgren Virginia Gun Range.

July 28, 1942

On the morning of the test, Captain Anderson, Lt. Price

and Wade Callahan climbed the steps of the control tower. Because the impact zone was 35,000 yards down range, it would require the gun to be at maximum elevation. Shells would leave the muzzle at 1400 feet per second, and reach a maximum height on over 36,000 feet before plunging down to the impact zone. In the test program, the first three shells had functional fuses, but no explosive charge. The last three standard armor piercing shells would have regular impact fuses, an explosive charge, and would impact 100 yards to the right of the first three. It took heavy equipment and a crew of miners to dig down to a depth of 200 feet to find the first three shells. The second three shells created 50 foot deep craters.

August 2, 1942

Based on the tests results, a high level War Department Meeting authorized a second comprehensive test that would simulate, as close as possible, the actual attack. Iowa would be used for the tests, and fire 200 special armor piercing rounds into an impact zone with three 500 foot deep wells in a geological formation similar to the actual Helium wells.

Finding a site for the tests proved difficult. There was nothing on the East Coast, and the only choice that had the right geology, and proximity to the ocean was near Coos Bay, Oregon. While the site would work, it was close enough to a populated area, for the sounds of the test firing to be heard by the population of the town, twenty miles South of the impact site.

August 7, 1942

Allied forces, predominantly United States Marines, land on Guadalcanal, Tulagi, and Florida in the southern Solomon Islands. Their objective is to deny the islands use by the Japanese to threaten Allied supply and communication routes between the United States, Australia, and New Zealand. Powerful American and Australian naval forces support these landings.

August 8,1942

In the naval Battle of Savo Island, near Guadalcanal, the Americans lose three cruisers, and the Australians one.

August 18, 1942

The Japanese reinforce New Guinea, and the Australians land troops at Port Moresby. Meanwhile, American planes have destroyed Japanese air power at Wewak, New Guinea.

August 20, 1942

Henderson Field on Guadalcanal receives its first American fighter planes.

Heavy equipment starts to cut an access road to the impact well site near Coos Bay, Oregon. The Navy announces they will be building a firing range on the site.

August 24, 1942

In the naval battle of the Eastern Solomons; the USS Enterprise is badly damaged and the Japanese lose one light carrier.

August 27, 1942

Marshal Zhukov, now partially recovered, is appointed to the command of the Stalingrad defense; the Luftwaffe is now delivering heavy strikes on the city.

A.G. Kimbrough

September 1, 1942

US Navy Construction Battalion personnel, Seabees, begin to arrive at Guadalcanal.

September 4, 1942

Manhattan Engineering District is formally created, and full-effort production of the atomic bomb components begins.

September 14, 1942

Japanese forces retreat again from Henderson Field, Guadalcanal.

Japanese forces are now within 30 miles of Port Moresby, New Guinea.

September 15, 1942

Americans send troops to Port Moresby as reinforcements for the Australian defenders.

Light carrier USS Wasp is sunk by a Japanese submarine off Guadalcanal.

September 23 to 27, 1942

In the Third Battle of Matanikau River, Guadalcanal, Japanese naval bombardment and landing forces nearly destroy Henderson Field in an attempt to take it. But, the attacking land forces are soon driven back.

October 11, 1942

On the Northwest coast of Guadalcanal, US Navy ships intercept and defeat a Japanese fleet on their way to reinforce troops on the island. With the help of Radar Fire Control they sink one cruiser and several Japanese destroyers.

October 12, 1942

The Red Army methods of ferrying troops across the Volga and into Stalingrad directly, seems to be a success, as the German advance comes to a halt.

October 18,1942

Admiral "Bull" Halsey is given command of the South Pacific naval forces.

November 12, 1942

A climactic naval battle near Guadalcanal starts between Japanese and American naval forces. Notably, the USS Juneau is sunk with the loss of much of its crew, including the five Sullivan brothers.

The Red Army makes an attempt to relieve Stalingrad at Kotelnikov, and is successful.

November 13, 1942

Aviators from the USS Enterprise sink the Japanese battleship Hiel.

November 14, 1942

The USS Washington sinks the Japanese battleship Kinshima using Radar Fire Control.

A.G. Kimbrough

November 15, 1942

The naval battle of Guadalcanal ends. Although the US Navy suffered heavy losses, it still retains control of the sea around Guadalcanal.

November 19, 1942

At Stalingrad, the Soviet Union forces under Marshal Zhukov launch Operation Uranus aimed at encircling the Germans in the city and thus turning the tide of battle in the USSR's favor.

November 21, 1942

The Red Army attempt at encirclement of Stalingrad continues, but stalls before it can complete the encirclement of the German Army. A 50 mile wide channel, the Cauldron, becomes a bloodbath, as both Armies throw men and equipment into the carnage.

American Army forces move to shove Japanese off the extreme Western end of Guadalcanal.

November 22, 1942

The situation for the German attackers of Stalingrad seems desperate. General Paulus sends Hitler a telegram saying that the German 6th Army will be surrounded, unless a strong relief force can help prevent a complete encirclement.

November 25, 1942

The attempted encirclement of Stalingrad continues, but heavy German bombing from Zeppelin Aircraft Carriers, and hastily mobilized forces from Poland manage to keep the gap open.

Hitler reiterates his demand of Paulus not to surrender.

December 1, 1942

Gasoline rationing begins in the United States.

The US cruiser Northampton is sunk by Japanese destroyers attempting to come down "the Slot" to Guadalcanal.

December 13, 1942

The Luftwaffe flies in meager supplies to the beleaguered Stalingrad troops. A massive relief Army is gathered from occupation forces all over Europe. A rail link is established that drops off troops, equipment, and supplies only twenty miles from the gap.

December 26, 1942

Heavy fighting continues on Guadalcanal, now focused on Mount Austen in the West.

January 10, 1943

Soviet troops launch an all-out offensive attack on Stalingrad; they also renew attacks in the North (Leningrad) and in the Caucasus, in spite of widespread ammunition and equipment shortages.

January 18, 1943

The Jews in the Warsaw Ghetto rise up for the first time, starting the Warsaw Ghetto Uprising.

The besieged defenders of Leningrad link up with

relieving forces.

January 28, 1943

A new conscription law in Germany states that men between sixteen and sixty-five and women between seventeen and fifty are open to mobilization.

The German reinforcement column reaches their forces outside Stalingrad, but the battle has broken the siege for the winter.

January 30, 1943

The last Japanese have cleared out of Guadalcanal by a brilliant evacuation plan undetected by the Americans.

February 7, 1943

In the United States, it is announced that shoe rationing will go into effect in two days.

February 9, 1943

Guadalcanal is finally secured; it is the first major achievement of the American offensive in the Pacific war.

February 22, 1943

USS Iowa, BB-61 is commissioned

March 1, 1943

U.S. and Australian naval forces, over three days, sink eight Japanese troop transports near New Guinea.

After The Days Of Infamy

March 10, 1943

The USAAF Fourteenth Air Force is formed in China, under General Chennault, former head of the "Flying Tigers".

March 11, 1943

The Germans enter Kharkov and the fierce struggle with the Red Army continues.

March 13, 1943

German forces liquidate the Jewish ghetto in Krakow.

March 28, 1943

With the US blockade on all shipping to or from Japan, the Helium supply in Germany is shrinking, and all operations of the Zeppelin Aircraft fleet are curtailed. The Zeppelin Corporation is directed to convert the Hindenburg to a liquid Helium tanker. It will be used exclusively to fly between Germany and Japan, with only a single refueling stop in South America. To maximize the cargo capacity, the diesel tanks are removed, and Propane will be used for fuel exclusively.

April 18, 1943

Admiral Yamamoto, chief architect of Japanese naval strategy, is killed when his plane is shot down by American P38's over Bougainville. He was on an inspection tour that US Navy code-breakers detect radio traffic announcing his schedule and destinations.

A.G. Kimbrough

May 2, 1943

Japanese aircraft again bomb Darwin Australia.

May 13, 1943

Remaining German Afrika Korps troops and equipment in North Africa are transferred to the Eastern Front, where the lines are stalled. Italian troops will take over all occupation duties.

May 15, 1943

The French underground forms an active "Resistance Movement." Their focus is disrupting the Vichy government and anything going to Germany.

May 16, 1943

The Warsaw Ghetto Uprising ends. The ghetto is destroyed, with about 14,000 Jews killed and about another 40,000 sent to the death camp at Treblinka.

June 3, 1943

The first Airship tanker run to Japan arrives in Tokyo, with four Special Government passengers.

Heinrich is in command of the Hindenburg, and he is looking forward to visiting with Rio, Mickey, and Gurti, while the two diplomats and two scientists are holding discussions with Japanese officials.

He is told their discussions will take a week, and that he should be ready to depart by then. The Government group had been unusually closed mouth about their mission, and the SS man in the crew, watched everyone like a hawk.

After The Days Of Infamy

During the middle of the week, the four friends have an enjoyable visit, and Mickey suggested that Heinrich bring Maria on the next trip, so she and Gurti could enjoy being together.

June 10, 1943

Instead of orders to depart, Heinrich is ordered to accompany the German officials to a meeting at the War Department. Before he left the hotel, the SS man told him the classification for the meeting is above the Top Secret clearance he already has.

When he walked into the meeting, he is surprised to see Mickey at the conference table.

Mickey was also summoned that morning. Besides Mickey, the only other person he recognized is now Admiral Minoru Genda.

By the end of the day, both men are shocked at the actions their governments are planning. The "Ultimate Solution" is a plan for the Japanese Airship fleet to fly over the North Pole and drop nerve gas bombs on a large portion of America's population centers. The two component nerve gas bombs had already been tested in a Northern China Provence. Two 500 pound bombs had been dropped from Army bombers at 10,000 feet. When the bombs reached 5000 feet, an explosion mixed the two compounds, creating a fog that slowly settled to the ground, Each bomb killed every living thing for fifty square miles.

The plan called for the Japanese Airship fleet to fly East after their North American bombing runs, where they would be refueled from tankers in mid-ocean, before proceeding to Germany. In Germany, the Airship Carriers would be refueled, and re-armed with German-built nerve

A.G. Kimbrough

gas bombs. At that point, the Japanese Airship Fleet, joined by the four Zeppelin Airship Carriers, carrying additional protective fighters, would bomb every industrial and population center in Russia.

The Japanese Airship Fleet would then return to Germany, refuel, and fly back to Japan.

The plan was developed in Germany when Hitler demanded a solution to the costly stalemate on the Eastern Front. It was approved by a Japanese Government that saw it as a way to knock America out of the war.

Germany needed the Japanese partnership because they only had four smaller Zeppelin Carriers and they needed the Japanese Airship Carriers to take out Russia in one strike. Japan needed the German assistance, because they were furnishing the bomb design and the means to refuel the fleet in the Atlantic.

The meetings continued over the next three days. Both Mickey and Heinrich were deeply disturbed, but kept those feelings to themselves. They could not accept the prospect of helping exterminate almost half the population of the civilized world. Each night, they met at Mickey's apartment for a private dinner, and discussed what they could do, even though any action would represent the highest form of treason. They parted, on the day Hindenburg was due to leave, with a commitment to do whatever it took to prevent this threat to humanity.

Mickey's participation in the Project, was to lead the design for the conversion of the airship fleet. The conversion would include:

Removal of all planes except for one fighter squadron for self defense.

Removal of all the gasoline storage tanks, pumps, and

plumbing systems, except for one to support the single fighter squadron.

Installation of gasbags to hold enough Propane fuel for a 10,000 mile flight.

Installation of storage and handling for ten, 1000 pound bombs that would drop out of the lower elevator.

Removal of all items not directly required for the mission, like crew cabins, defensive machine guns, and unneeded sections of the hanger deck.

Removal of the Helium recovery system.

Mickey estimated it would take a minimum of six months to complete the modifications on all four Airships. In a meeting at the Hokkaido airship base, Mickey learned that a factory was being built nearby. It would be building the components and the Nerve Gas bomb assemblies.

Heinrich's responsibilities included oversight of the logistics to support all phases of the project, including insuring enough liquid Helium to refill the German Zeppelin Aircraft Carriers, and top off the Japanese Aircraft Carriers. He would make two trips to Japan in the Hindenburg, every month, until the project is executed.

June 21, 1943

Operation Cartwheel opened with landings by the United States Fourth Marine Raider Battalion at Segi Point on New Georgia in the Solomon Islands.

June 23, 1943

American troops landed in the Trobriand Islands, close to New Guinea. The American strategy of driving up the Southwest Pacific by "Island Hopping" continued.

June 30, 1943

The Hindenburg returns to Tokyo. Heinrich joins Mickey and Rio for a quiet dinner at Mickey's apartment.

The plotters realize that they must act quickly in order for the Americans have time to take countermeasures. Heinrich has developed a plan to take control of the Hindenburg on his next flight back from Tokyo. He will bring Maria as a cabin attendant, and suggests Mickey fly his Storch, with Rio and Gurti on board. They can land on the Zeppelin, and enter through the top hatch, after sending a false distress call.

After refueling in South America, they will fly the Hindenburg to America and warn them about the impending attack. Their combined knowledge should be invaluable in helping the Americans develop a way to prevent Japan and Germany from killing half the population of the civilized world.

Rio has terminated critical maintenance schedules in the Processing Plant, and destroyed all of the plant detailed construction plans.

Mickey has already started sabotaging several different items in the Airship modifications, including introducing a mathematical error in the fuel consumption calculations.

July 1, 1943

The Hindenburg departs Tokyo with the plotter's plans in motion.

July 7, 1943

Walter Dornberger briefs Hitler on the V-2 Rocket status. Hitler delays the production project because there is no immediate need for this super weapon, the economy is failing, and the available resources must be directed to the Eastern Front and the "Ultimate Solution Project" He authorizes the engineering team to proceed with development of the next generation A4 rocket, and it's mobile transporter.

July 10, 1943

The Hindenburg departs Germany with Maria on board as a cabin attendant. There are also four Government Officials on board, including a high level SS officer. The balance of the crew have been carefully selected by Heinrich to include single men with a high degree of personal loyalty to him.

July 14, 1943

The Hindenburg lands in Tokyo, and begins refueling and loading helium. Mickey is alarmed when he overhears the SS man tell one of the other passengers he will review all the Kempeitai security procedures and records for anyone connected with the Project.

Heinrich and Marie have dinner with Mickey, Gurti, and Rio on the second evening. Heinrich tells them about a letter he received just before he left Germany. It was from Wade Callahan, who reported that he and Hekoi are well and happily living in Northern Virginia. They are expecting their first child, and he is working as a civilian for the US Navy. Everyone is thrilled that the couple made it to safety, and agreed that the US Government now knew about the existence and location of the Helium wells and processing plant.

They discuss the final details of their escape plan. The

next day, Gurti takes Maria shopping, and Maria purchases many items, including antiques and a large china collection. She arranges to have them shipped on the next helium tanker flight that does not have the weight of extra passengers.

July 16, 1943

The Hindenburg departs from Tokyo on a clear morning. Rio, Mickey, and Gurti are at the airport and join several hundred officials to say goodbye. When the Zeppelin is airborne, the remaining plotters walk over to the hanger where Mickey's Storch is waiting. Gurti has a photographic hobby and has been snapping pictures of the activities all morning.

Mickey has told his secretary he planned to fly after the Zeppelin so that his wife can take pictures of the Hindenburg with the Japanese mainland in the background.

When both craft are airborne, the conspirators feel great relief.

The Storch follows the Hindenburg until both craft are fifty miles off-shore, and there are no other aircraft or ships in sight. At that point, a hatch opened on the Hindenburg control cabin, and five bodies tumble out.

Gurti gasped, and Mickey replied, "Those are the Nazis, who were on board. It's now time to make my first airship landing."

The Zeppelin slows from its ninety mile per hour cruising speed, and the Storch matched its speed. The Stortz approaches the landing platform on the top of the airship. Foot by foot it reached the small platform, where four burly crewmen wait. When the wheels touch, the crewmen lock them to the platform as the airship loses speed.

Mickey releases the canopy, and it sailed away because he had removed the locks. Two crewmen helped Gurti out of the cockpit, and down through the access hatch. At that point, Micky activated the Emergency channel radio and broadcasts a distress message reporting an engine fire, and cut it off just as he started to give a position. This action, coupled with what his secretary would report, plus the purchases Maria made, should present a believable picture of their loss at sea.

The crewmen return, and help Rio down. He stopped at the hatch and watched Mickey increase the throttle, and climb out of the cockpit. As soon as he is clear, the other two crewmen release the wheel locks, and the Stortz lifts off the platform. It rises a few feet before dipping one wing and disappearing.

Heinrich and Maria are waiting at the bottom of the hatch, and escort them down to the bridge, where a bottle of chilled champagne is waiting for them to celebrate their new freedom.

July 18, 1943

The fuel stop in South America was brief, and no one left the Hindenburg during the three hours they are attached to the mooring mast.

At dusk, 200 miles offshore, Heinrich broadcasts a message. "Mayday, Mayday, Mayday, this is the Zeppelin Hindenburg. We have an uncontrolled fire, and are going down."

After dropping off two burned life jackets, the Hindenburg turns to the Northwest.

A.G. Kimbrough

July 19, 1943 0730

The sun is rising as the Hindenburg approaches the Texas border, just southwest of El Paso. Heinrich switches on the radio transmitter to the International Aircraft Emergency Frequency, "Attention, this is the Zeppelin Hindenburg. I am declaring an in-flight emergency. We are 20 miles Southwest of the Fort Bliss Airfield. Please restrict air traffic, and have a ground crew ready to take our mooring lines."

Hindenburg did not respond to the tower's increasing demands for more information.

July 19, 1943 0800

The shadows are gone from the field when the Hindenburg approaches, thirty minutes later. There are several men on the field, ready to grab the trailing lines. There are also several mobile antiaircraft guns positioned along the runway, and a dozen jeeps filled with MPs.

Rio commented, "Even though the US is not at war with Germany, I hope the swastikas on the tail don't start anyone shooting."

Soon, the ground-crew grab the two mooring lines, and secure each one to a heavy truck that ran on to the field when the mooring lines are in hand. Then the trucks drive between the two largest hangers, pulling the Zeppelin with them. The mooring line winches slowly pull the airship down, as some Helium is vented, stopping when the gondola is 25 feet off the ground. Then the elevator slowly comes down, with Heinrich, Maria, Mickey, Gurti, and Rio as the only passengers.

An Army Air Corps Bird Colonel, meets them. He is surrounded by a ring of MPs with drawn weapons. After ten minutes of tense discussions, they are escorted to an office building behind the largest hanger.

Rio acted as the spokesman and said, "So you see Colonel Thomas, we are all three graduates of the 1929 UCLA class, and have stayed in contact since then. Our escape from Germany and Japan was triggered, because we became aware of a serious threat to your nation, and most of the rest of humanity. Even though our actions will be considered traitorous by our homelands, we cannot stand to do nothing.

We have an American friend, who spent several years in Japan, before we helped him escape the clutches of the Kempeitai. He is now working for the US Navy, for the people who need the knowledge he has about his activities in Japan. Those same people will need the critical information we bring. Please contact Mr. Wade Callahan, as quickly as possible, because time is urgent."

Rio continued, "Our crewmen are all volunteers, and not enemy combatants. Please treat them as civilians. We came to this base because it's isolation, and it's critical that you keep the presence of Hindenburg secret. I suggest you place camouflage nets over it. The ship is the property of the Zeppelin Company, and not the German Government. She is loaded with enough liquid Helium to keep the German fleet of airship carriers operational for six months.

July 19, 1943 1100

Wade Callahan had just signed for the shipment of drill bits for the Coos Bay Test site. He was planning to load them as cargo on the B-25, and fly them out that afternoon. The Office Manager at the Houston drill bit company called him to the phone, and said, "Some guy in Washington needs to talk to you, and says it's urgent."

Wade picked up the phone, and heard Lt. Price's voice. "Wade. Is that you?"

"Yes, it's me, What's going on? I thought you would be working at the farm this weekend."

Price replied, "They called me in. Something urgent came up. I can't say much on the phone, but you need to fly over to the Fort Bliss Airfield at El Paso, as soon as you can get there. Some of your old friends are waiting to see you. I need you to take them here. We can talk on the secure line at the base. I'll be waiting for your call."

Wade is puzzled, but he arranges for the drill bits to ship by air, and drives back to the airport. The plane assigned to him was a refurbished B-25. An Army General had ordered it, so he and his staff could fly in comfort. It is outfitted with a bar, sound proofing, padded leather seating for eight, and a restroom. The General is not happy, but the needs of Project Javelin have a much higher priority than the needs of the Supply Corps General.

July 19, 1943 1730

Just before touchdown, Wade noticed the tail of a Zeppelin between two hangers. It had a camouflage net over it, but he still recognized it, and understood who his mysterious friends might be.

Colonel Thomas, the Base Commander, was waiting when Wade left the B-25. "Mr. Callahan, I don't know who you are, but you have friends in very high places. I'm ordered by the Secretary of the Army Air Corps to give you anything you want, with no questions asked. I also had a message from a Lt. Price to have you call him right away, using my secure phone line."

The Colonel took him over to his office, pointed at the

red phone on his desk, and left the room, closing the door on his way out.

Wade dialed the number, and Elmer answered, "You made good time. Have you figured out who your friends are?"

"When I saw the Zeppelin tail, I had an idea. Who is here besides Heinrich?"

"Rio, Mickey, Gurti, and Maria. They stole the Hindenburg as it left Tokyo. We need them here as soon as possible. Rio says he has urgent news about a major threat, that he will only discuss with you."

Wade answered, "We can leave as soon as they finish refueling our plane."

Elmer said. "It will be late when you get here. I'll have transportation waiting for you, to bring everyone out to my place. The big house has plenty of room, security, and our wives can look after Gurti and Maria, tomorrow, while we all go to DC.

After Wade hung up, the Colonel took him to a conference room. Before he entered, Wade asked the Colonel to have dinner for the flight crew, his guests, and himself, taken out to his plane, since they would be flying most of the night. He also asked to have the plane's fuel tanks topped off.

The reunion was heartfelt, but guarded, since they all suspected the conference room might be bugged. Ten minutes later, they were boarding the plane.

During the four hour flight, Wade learned the broad scope of the Ultimate Solution Project. Mickey asked Gurti to transcribe their discussions, since she was a skilled secretary, who could take shorthand.

A.G. Kimbrough

Wade is staggered by the implications of what he hears, and tells his friends they may have saved most of the world's population. He radioed Price and tells him to have paper and a portable typewriter in the car, when they land.

On the way to the farm from the airport, Gurti starts typing up the notes of their in-flight discussions. Price reads each page as it is finished. They are pulling up the drive to the big house as Price read the last page. He called his security chief over and says, "Have this taken to the White House for immediate copying and distribution, classified above Top Secret."

July 20, 1943

It was a day filled with high level meetings. Project Javelin took on an even higher priority, with a Presidential directive that the schedule must accelerate to the maximum degree. Rio, Mickey, and Heinrich are given Project Javelin security clearances, civilian job classifications, and will work in the same farm office as Wade and Elmer. The Secret Service takes over security for the Project staff and the farm, where they will continue to live and work for the duration.

Over the next three weeks, the primary objective of Project Javelin shifts. While destruction of the Helium wells and processing plant would force the Airship Carriers to switch to Hydrogen lift gas, and increase their vulnerability to tracers, it will not prevent the launch of the Ultimate Solution attacks.

Since the location of the Airship base, and the nerve gas bomb factory are now known, the only viable near-term approach, is to attack those sites with the Iowa. If she attacks, and destroys the Airship base, and the nerve gas plant first, she could then move back along the coast thirty

124

miles, and destroy the Helium wells and processing plant.

A serious problem with the additional targets, is the extended time close to the Hokkaido coast, which will significantly increase the likelihood Iowa will come under air attack from ground based aircraft. There is no other Battleship available that can match Iowa's AA defenses, or speed.

The original attack plan called for two carriers to stop 300 miles off-shore, and launch fighter squadrons as soon as Iowa started her retreat. Now the plan is revised to include a third carrier, even though it will stop the convoy traffic to Hawaii. All three carriers will carry the newest generation Corsair fighters. The Corsairs will be equipped with drop tanks that would allow them to remain over the Iowa almost an hour.

Under the revised plan. the Carriers will approach to within 200 miles, even though some think the mission could result in major ship and plane losses. While the Iowa could be considered expendable, losing even a single carrier would be catastrophic to the Pacific war effort.

The original project time line had to remain, because the January Arctic storms would give the best opportunity to approach Hokkaido without detection. Unfortunately, those same storms would make it difficult to safely recover the fighters returning from protecting the Iowa.

August 5, 1943

The newcomers are settled in the newly completed cottages and the ladies are getting along well. The pool and soaking tub are used frequently, but Helen and Hekoi agreed to forgo any nudity until later.

A.G. Kimbrough

September 3, 1943

Director Kelley called Lt. Price, and asked him to bring Mr, Callahan over to his office when they returned from lunch. The request wasn't unusual, since it happened every other day.

Director Kelley told them to sit down, and said, "I had breakfast with the President this morning, and he gave me another assignment. He worries about the potential political backlash that could occur when we disclose Project Javelin, after keeping it away from most of Congress, and the American public. He directed me to find a competent Photo Journalist, get them cleared, and hire them for the duration, to record and describe the entire project, from beginning to end, even if it fails."

"I'm passing the buck to you two. There has to be airtight security, so you have to pick someone willing to cut all ties for the duration. They will have to live out at the farm, I believe you can add another cottage without a problem. It would probably be best if the person wasn't married, so a spouse wouldn't have to be locked down. You can offer them double whatever salary they are making, in addition to having their byline on the biggest story of the war."

After a few questions, Wade and Elmer returned to their DC office. Price shook his head, and remarked, "I don't know why he picked us for this job, they should have given it to somebody in the Office of Public Relations . We know nothing about Journalism."

Wade replied, "No one over there has the clearance to talk about Javelin. We need to run out to the office at the farm. I have an idea I need to talk to Rio about."

To avoid any talk about German and Japanese working

in DC, the Sea Bees erected a large Quonset hut at the farm, and set it up as offices for the Javelin team.

In route to the farm, Wade explained his idea to Elmer. An hour later, they walked into the Office building, and Wade asked Rio to come into the office that he and Elmer shared. Elmer did not join them, and Wade closed the door, which was unusual.

Rio looked surprised, and said, "What have I done wrong now?"

"Nothing, I just need to have a discussion which is personal. How well do you know Betty Lawrence?"

Rio got a shocked look on his face, and said, "You know she was my girlfriend for two years at UCLA. You also know I spent three weeks with her when she was in Tokyo to cover the first visit of the Hindenburg, and yes, we slept together every night. Is this something to do with my security clearance?"

Wade replied, "No, we have a new assignment, direct from the President, to hire a Photo Journalist to document the Javelin Project. We are considering her for that assignment. It will require her to live here at the farm. She will be confined for the duration, just like you three. Will you have a problem working closely with her for the duration?"

Rio smiled and said, "I have no problem, unless there is a rule against project team members being intimate. I plan to ask her to be my wife the next time I see her."

Wade laughed, and said, "I'll take that as a yes. The FBI is vetting her as we speak. If they give her a green light, I'll be asking her to join our team.

A.G. Kimbrough

September 10, 1943

The FBI agent handed the report to Lt. Price, and said, "She is clean, except for a couple of things. She had a two-year affair with a Japanese national named Rio Watanabe, who was attending UCLA, in 1928 and 1929. She also was in Tokyo to cover the arrival of the first flight of the Zeppelin Hindenburg. After it departed, she spent three weeks with Watanabe, before her passenger liner departed for the states.

"The lady has enjoyed a number of overnight relationships with several different men and women over the years."

Price smiled and replied, "For reasons beyond you security clearance, the contacts with Mr. Watanabe are not a problem. We will accept your vetting for our requirements. Thanks for all your efforts. I'll send a letter confirming our acceptance, with Director Kelley's signature."

Later that afternoon, he called Betty Lawrence at her Movietone office.

"This is Lt. Price of the Office of Naval Intelligence, is this Betty Lawrence?"

"Yes, what can I do for the Navy today?"

"I would like to have you meet me for a critical meeting tomorrow morning. I'm sorry for the short notice, but the matter is urgent."

She questioned, "Can you tell me what this is about?"

"I'm sorry, the subject is classified, and I can't mention it over an open telephone line. I can have a car waiting at your apartment at 9:00 AM. I'll be able to answer most of your questions when we are face to face. Will you be ready at that time?"

Betty replied, "I don't know what this is all about, but I'll see you in the morning."

September 12, 1943

Betty was surprised to see the olive green Cadillac pull up to her Georgetown apartment.

Elmer was sure he had to do a sales job on her, and he hoped using the Director's car would be a good start. While she had seen and interviewed lots of VIPs, she had never ridden in a Cadillac before. The sailor driving was polite, but did not give her any new information.

An older then she expected, Lt. was waiting at the curb. He introduced himself as Lt. Price, and took her to a conference room on the third floor. After she declined his offer of coffee or a cold drink, he sat down across the table from her.

"We have a lot to cover today, and I suggest we speak informally. Please call me Elmer, and may I call you Betty?"

"Of course Elmer, I always try to conduct my interviews informally."

Elmer smiled, and said. "There is one formality we need to get out of the way before we can proceed. Because of this project's extreme security classification, I must have you read and sign this document."

He opened a folder, and handed it to her, along with a Parker pen.

Betty started reading, and quickly found that she could be tried for treason, if she disclosed anything she learned during the day. She had often had to sign confidentiality agreements before an interview would be granted, but this was serious. Her opinion about the critical nature of the project, was increasing, and she realized that her participation could be important. She no longer thought her participation would be as a PR hack.

After carefully reading through all four pages of the document, she signed it. Betty closed the folder, handed it back to Elmer, and said, "I think I'll take that cup of coffee before we continue. This really is serious."

Elmer brought a tray containing two plain white "Navy" cups, two spoons, a Thermos bottle full of coffee, plus cream, and sugar. After pouring both their cups, he sat down and said. "That is the worst part for today. I will describe what your participation in the project would be, and the reason we need someone of your capability as part of the team."

"President Roosevelt directed this office to bring on a Photo Journalist to tell the story of a project, that if successful, can save most humanity from a looming disaster. Because of the extreme threat, He has kept the threat and our attempt to counter it, from the American people, much of Congress, most of the government, and military. If any news of our knowledge of the threat, or planned countermeasures should leak, those countermeasures will fail."

"Success of this project will remove the threat and help end the war, while failure will result in the few survivors becoming slaves. When the threat is removed, the President wants to release an objective story that thoroughly documents the history of this project, including the people that make it happen. If we fail, that history may only be a historical footnote somewhere."

"If you choose to join this team, you will need to take an unpaid leave of absence from Movietone, telling them you will work on a classified government project. You will become a civilian employee at a salary that is double what you presently earn. The report that you create will be issued to the public under your byline. It will be the most important news story of the war."

The security restrictions placed on you, and the rest of the project team are severe. You will live in nearby secure facility under guard by the Secret Service, and the FBI. You may not have direct contact with family, friends, or former co-workers. The facility is a 200 acre horse farm, and the living conditions are not severe. I live there with my wife and children, and they love it. We have a communal dining room, with a great chef, an indoor pool and gymnasium, first run movies, and plenty of outdoor recreational opportunities. You will have an on site office, with other senior members of the team.

"Your assignment may last through the duration of the war. Realistically, even if we achieve success, the war may go on for a few more years."

The pair spent the balance of the day, except for a brief break to eat a sandwich and drink a Coke, with Betty asking questions, and Elmer answered all those he could. There were many he could not answer until Betty officially joined the team.

By 5:00 PM, the discussions were completed, and still Elmer had not asked Betty for a commitment. He looked at his watch, and said, "I'm sure you have noticed that I haven't asked you to make a commitment yet. I want you to come back here tomorrow, after thinking about it tonight. I know it is a decision you won't make lightly. Assuming your decision tomorrow is affirmative, then I'll take out to the facility to meet the team."

Betty rode the Cadillac back to her apartment, ate a

light supper, and made a stiff drink. She drank it down, made another, and took a long, hot shower. Afterward, she climbed in bed, sipped her drink, and wondered, "What in the hell are you getting yourself into, girl?"

With no close family members, or current boyfriend, and only a few girlfriends, her professional life so far, had prevented her from acquiring many strings. Movietone might not allow her to have a leave of absence, but with a report commissioned by the President, she wouldn't have to worry about employment. Betty fell asleep, still thinking about her decision.

September 13, 1943

Elmer was waiting at the curb when she stepped out of the Cadillac. He smiled and said, "If you have decided to not to join the team, you can go back home now."

Betty smiled, closed the Cadillac door, and replied, "I'm not sure what I'm getting into, but I'm in."

Elmer laughed and said, "That's probably the last Cadillac ride you'll have for a while." He took off his hat and waved it. An olive green Ford pulled up to the curb. A tough looking guy in a suit was at the wheel.

The man got out, and looked all around, while Elmer and Betty got into the back seat. Betty noticed a bulge in the man's shoulder which showed he is carrying a gun.

Elmer mentioned, "This is Walter, and he is with the Secret Service, who provide the inner layer of Security for the Project team. We are going out to the Farm so you can meet the rest of the Team."

Conversation was limited to small talk after Betty started to ask a question about the Project, and Elmer tightly closed his lips and shook his head no.

After The Days Of Infamy

The entrance gate was manned by a pair of armed US Marines, who opened it after checking Elmer's ID. The narrow road led over a hill into a valley with a large house and several outbuildings at the opposite end. On one side of the house were three Quonset huts, and they parked in front of the middle one.

They entered, a long, unoccupied hall, and stopped in front of a door marked Conference Room. Elmer put his hand on the doorknob and said, "You know some of these folks."

Betty stepped into the room and was shocked to see Mickey. Rio, Heinrich, and another man seated at the table. She turned to Elmer and said, "Why didn't you tell me?"

Elmer replied. "The presence of these men in the United States is highly classified. In fact, it is the reason for Project Javelin's existence. The man you don't know is Wade Callahan, who discovered the helium gas deposit, and escaped from Japan before the war started. We will spend the balance of today telling you the rest of the story."

They broke for lunch, and walked over to the next Quonset hut, which had a small canteen. They were the only occupants and started getting seated at the only table.

Rio walked up to Betty after she sat down, dropped to one knee, and said, "Betty Lawrence, I'm so glad you came back into my life. Please say you will let me make you my wife."

Betty's response was unexpected. Tears appeared in her eyes, and she replied, "I'm so honored by your request, and I would be pleased to share your bed and be your lover for as long as you want me. But I can't agree to be your wife, and have a monogamous married relationship with you.

"Since we first met, I have learned a lot about myself. I

133

am a sexual person, who, after an early life miscarriage left me unable to have children. Since then, I have enjoyed a wide range of male and female sexual partners. Because I am easily sexually attracted to others, and will not be in a relationship, where responding to that attraction would be cheating on my relationship partner.

"I'm sorry, Rio, but I would never want to do anything that could hurt you.

The room went silent when she started speaking. Betty looked around, and fled through the door of the women's Rest Room.

After a moment, Elmer walked backed to his Office and made a phone call to his wife Helen.

Helen Price came from old money. Her grandfather had been a Virginia Senator. She met Elmer in college and fell in love. Elmer was an enlisted man then, and way below her station. Her immediate family attempted to dissuade her from marriage. She told them she didn't give a damn about their threat to disinherit her, and became Mrs. Price. Her grandfather didn't give a damn about his daughter's disapproval, and left the Farm and most of his wealth, to Helen.

A half hour later, Helen knocked, and entered the restroom where Betty was attempting to pull herself together. After an hour of frank discussions, both women left the restroom. When they entered the conference room, there were three other women seated at the table.

Helen turned to Betty and said, "I called these ladies in, because they need to hear what we have to say. This is Maria, Mrs. Lehmann, and Mickey's wife is Gurti, who is Heinrich's little sister. Wade Calender's wife is Hekoi."

Helen spoke, "Ladies and Gentlemen, we have a

problem that must be addressed here and now. The problem can destroy the ability of this team to work together as we must, to achieve success. Rio, inadvertently, forced Betty to effectively strip herself naked before you fellows, in order to be true to her own morality, and to be fair to a man she thinks the world of.

All of us have done things we don't want in the public record. This team is living and operating in the highest security ever imagined. It has forced us to be a family, and it needs to have no secrets between us. Who are we to judge Betty's life, or sexuality. I challenge each of you to follow my example and show our expanded family has no judgments, or secrets."

Elmer had been watching his wife, and had no idea what she had in mind. He had asked her to talk to Betty, get her calmed down, and willing to return to the meeting.

Helen remaining standing and said, "Tonight, after dinner, everyone is invited to join us at the pool for a swim and a soak, Both Betty and myself will not be wearing swimming suits, which will be optional. We have no secrets with this family, including our naked bodies."

Rio walked over to Betty, and said, "Darling, I love you, and acknowledge that we are both free to have sex with others of our choice. We are sexual beings and I'm willing to share, without reservations."

Betty turned to the ladies and said, "One thing I want to be absolutely clear on, is the fact that even if I'm attracted to someone. If they are in a relationship, I would never act on that attraction, without a face to face approval from the other person in that relationship. I would never knowingly do anything to harm someone's relationship. I will be in a relationship with Rio, but he has my permission to have a sexual relationship with anyone."

Betty then turned and hugged and kissed Rio deeply.

Elmer embraced Helen, and thanked her for her actions. Then she embraced Rio while Betty embraced Elmer.

The process repeated until all the ladies had embraced and kissed everyone. The room filled with sexual tension, wonderment, and a developing bond among the group.

Wade took a deep breath, and said, "I suggest that it's time to get to work. We have a lot to cover today. We can resume our bonding tonight after dinner Thanks to you ladies, this has been both enlightening and fulfilling.

During the balance of the afternoon, Betty is given an overview of the team's history and culminated with the disclosure of the Ultimate Solution's threat to humanity.

When the meeting broke up at 5:30 PM, Rio walked across the street with her to the cottage that would be her new home. During the day the Secret Service had moved everything into it from her apartment. It had a small kitchen, a setting room, bedroom, and a bathroom with a claw-foot tub. The couple made love on her bed, before Rio returned to his adjacent cottage to dress for dinner. Betty took a long, hot, bubble bath, and marveled at the path her life was taking.

The other couples took advantage of the time after the meeting broke up and before going to dinner for love making, and a lot of frank discussions.

Dinner was in the Big House Dinning Room, and started at 7:00 PM. The dinner conversation did not include anything about the project because that subject is forbidden, away from the office, or other secure locations. The chef, Benton Williams had been with the family since Helen was a child. He lived with his wife Clara, in a basement apartment. They were not read in on the project, although both had been fully vetted by the FBI.

The dinner conversations were more of a personal nature, and helped Betty to get to know the people of the project team. Elmer and Helen had a girl, eleven and a thirteen years old son. Wade and Hekoi had a eleven month-old daughter. The children had been fed, and were under Clara's watchful eye in the upstairs playroom.

Helen admitted to being a wild child as a young woman, who was thankful she had not become pregnant or infected during that time. She met Elmer in college, and resolved to seduce him. Since he was a sailor, the seduction was not difficult. By the next morning, she admitted that she was in love with him. They were married three months later, over her families objections. She was pregnant six months afterwards.

The team learned that Betty was born in Nebraska, and her parents were deceased. She told of selling the family farm when she graduated from High School, and taking the bus to LA, in an attempt to be discovered by a Hollywood agent. She had been there a year, working as a movie usher when she met Mickey, Heinrich, and Rio at a party. There was a mutual attraction with Rio, and she went home with him that night. She kept working, and her small rented room, still hopeful of being discovered, but spent most nights with Rio.

Marie and Hekoi were curious about Heinrich's and Mickey's activities after Betty mentioned the occasional skinny dipping parties. Betty told them they would have to talk to those guys about their UCLA activities.

After prodding, both guys admitted sowing more than a few wild oats with the young women who were happy to attend a wild Beverly Hills party. They were a mix of wannabe starlets, showgirls, and UCLA students.

After Rio left, Betty continued trying to be discovered. She landed a couple of bit parts after sleeping with a Producer. He dropped her like a stone when she became pregnant and made the decision to have the baby.

She accepted the fact that as a single mother, there was no possibility she could break into show business. A school in LA offered a one year's course in Photo Journalism, and she spent the rest of her savings to pay the tuition.

The stress of everything led to a miscarriage, with serious complications, and she almost died. After she left the hospital, the operation that saved her life, had left her sterilized. She found her apartment repossessed, and her possessions sold to pay for the overdue rent.

The school allowed her to start her course at the next semester, and she hung on, working two jobs, and renting a room at a cheap boarding house. When the school started, there wasn't time to work enough hours to make ends meet.

Betty had avoided several offers to exchange sexual favors for cash in the past, but it became a necessity to earn enough cash to survive in the few hours available between sleep and school.

Her success, as a high dollar call girl developed quickly. She had the numbers of most guys who had offered to pay, and her enthusiastic sexual appetite and good looks made her a favorite. Those client referrals allowed her to avoid a pimp, or the need to hang out in hotel bars.

By the time she finished school, Betty had $10,000 in the bank, and faced a decision about her future. The movie industry had soured for her, and to stay in LA would likely keep her in prostitution. One of her teachers, who was also a friend, suggested that she go to New York, where most of the Newsreel companies were located. Her diploma, and good looks should help get an interview.

A week later, she was on the train headed for the Big Apple. Movietone News was the third company she interviewed, and they made an offer at the end of the interview. The man who interviewed her was also a graduate from the same LA school as she attended. He became her boss, and in the second month, failed to seduce her. After her experience with the Hollywood Producer, she resolved to never mix sex with her business associates. The boss was disappointed, but she had the potential to become the best Photo Journalist on the staff.

By the time she joined the Javelin Project, Betty was the top reporter on the Movietone staff, and had her pick of assignments. She had enjoyed a wide range of lovers, from business, politics, Broadway, the military, and a even couple of Doctors.

Maria reported that she had been raised in a strict Catholic home, but had been raped by a priest when she was fifteen. Even though he tried to convince her she should feel honored God selected her to give him relief, she didn't believe him. She never went back to the church, even though her family tried to force her, saying she would burn forever in hell. She ran away from home a year later and joined a group of Spanish Civil War partisans. A woman in the group took her in, and they had an affair that lasted until the woman was killed.

She met and fell in love with a German pilot in the closing days of the war in Spain. They were married, just before he was due to return to Germany.

Heinrich was the first man she made love to since her husband Rolf was killed in the war. She is in love with him, and their sex life is great. Maria admitted that the embraces this afternoon had excited her.

Hekoi confessed that she didn't understand the reason some people found nudity upsetting. In Japan, it was not uncommon for adults to bathe in the presence of other, unrelated adults. While most Japanese married women were monogamous, it was common knowledge that most Japanese married men were not. She then said she didn't think it was fair, in this modern day, because, in America, unlike Japan, women were not second class citizens.

Wade protested he had always been faithful, but she cut him off, stating that she wasn't accusing him. She said she was just talking about what was fair.

Gurti asserted that mixed nudity was not uncommon in Europe, and that many couples had lovers outside marriage, usually without their partner's knowledge.

When dinner was finished by 9:00 PM, everyone went to the changing rooms, where towels and robes were hanging in the lockers.

Helen led Betty to the far lockers, and while they were disrobing, whispered, "Elmer and I talked about having you spend the night with us. We would love to have you join both of us, if you are interested. We're both excited at the prospect."

Betty replied, "That sounds like fun, I've never done a threesome before. I fucked Rio to a parade rest this afternoon. And I suspect he'll be ready to go to sleep before long. I'll tell him I have other plans for later."

Everyone wore their robes to the pool, and dropped them at the edge. Then the guys all dove in, while the ladies took their time, and enjoyed the view. Since the pool water is cool, soon everyone was in the hot tub. The discussions were uninhibited, but careful, and touches were restricted to significant partners.

By 10:00 PM, the pool party was breaking up, and soon, only Betty, Elmer, and Helen were still in the hot tub. Helen embraced Betty, and said, "I can't wait any more. Lets go up to bed. Elmer has a stiffy, just waiting for you, and I want to watch."

September 14, 1943

Even though the night had featured little sleep, Betty rose at dawn and returned to her cottage. She took another long hot bath, dressed in a business suit, and had a pot of tea, while she listened to the early news on her radio.

The meetings started at 9:00 AM, and continued for the next two days. At that point, Wade and Elmer left for the West Coast. Wade would oversee the Test Site construction near Coos Bay Oregon. Elmer would go to the Long Beach Naval Shipyard, where the Iowa would be receiving upgrades to the Fire Control Computers. None of the crew, including the Captain, had any idea about their participation in Project Javelin.

September 15, 1943

Chiang Kai-sheck asked that General Stilwell, American military adviser/commander, be recalled for suggesting an alliance with the Communists.

September 16, 1943

Sea Bees relocate the security offices in the third Quonset Hut to a new building at the outside gate. They strip back the Quonset Hut interior to an open space, and equip it as a model shop. Two large tables become the base of scale models of the Helium wells and Processing Plant, the Airship Base, and the Nerve Gas Bomb Factory.

Rio and Mickey become the primary model makers, with the help of a well vetted, small Navy team of craftsmen, mapmakers, and artists.

Heinrich spends most days in DC with a Navy team charged with developing detailed information on both the German and Japanese airships technology and operations. Since Mickey is restricted to the farm, Heinrich acts as an information conduit between him and the Navy team. Eventually, the two will collaborate on a cutaway scale model of a Japanese airship carrier.

September 17, 1943

When the older Lt. arrives at the Quarter Deck, and asks to see the Captain, the ten-year younger Lt. OOD is skeptical, until Elmer showed him a letter signed by Admiral King, the Chief of Naval Operations.

Captain John Baker had not been scheduled to take command of the Iowa, until her construction schedule was moved up. The original Captain Designate was on the Staff of Admiral Gromley in the South Pacific, and the Admiral refused to release him early.

Captain Baker had been scheduled to command a new Atlanta Class Cruiser because he was considered an expert in antiaircraft defense. The Iowa was a different beast, and he relished the prospect of taking her to war.

He is surprised to see Price in his office. He did know about his actions on the Fletcher, against the Airship Carriers. Baker didn't understand the letter from King ordering him to give Price anything he needed at a maximum priority. The only thing the letter said was that Price would oversee some Fire Control Computer modifications and a future weapons test. It also classified everything Price would do at Above Top Secret.

Captain Baker assigned Price a stateroom and an office normally occupied by the Flag Lieutenant.

September 21, 1943

The battle of the Solomons is now considered at an unofficial end.

September 22, 1943

Australian forces land at Finschafen, a small port in New Guinea. The Japanese will continue the battle well into October.

September 23, 1943

Heinrich returns to the Farm accompanied by Admiral King and Howard Hughes. Hughes had been hammering Congress and the Navy Department for months, with his ideas for building wooden framed airship aircraft carriers.

When Admiral King asked Halsey about the idea, Halsey replied "Why in the hell aren't you already building them? The Japs can hit anywhere because they are so mobile, and the Airship Carriers should be faster to build than a Fleet Carrier."

The same day, King authorized Hughes to be read in on Project Javelin, and given access to it's airship experts. King also took funding for three new Jeep carriers that couldn't start construction until drydock space was available, and directed those funds to be used to design and build two wooden airship carriers capable of holding at least 100 planes.

The meeting that afternoon results in Mickey and Heinrich being assigned to lead the airship carrier design team, which will be based in a new building right there on the Farm. The airships will use the same basic design as the Japanese airships, except that spruce and birch will be used instead of bamboo, and nylon fabric instead of silk

With the signed development contract in hand Hughes, forms a team with Goodyear-Zeppelin to manufacture the new Airship Carriers. The assembly will be based at the site of a former furniture manufacturing plant, in the countryside near Raleigh, North Carolina. When the airship carriers join the fleet, they will bring the ability to strike anywhere in the world.

September 25, 1943

The Red Army retakes Smolensk.

September 26, 1943

Wade Callahan arrived at Point Magu Naval Air Station for Airborne Gunnery Spotting training.

The Iowa Senior Pilot, Lt. Rodney Marks was not happy with being sent TAD to train a damned civilian. Marks had hoped to take a week leave while the ship was in the yard. The guy was on some kind of super secret Project, and would be actually doing the spotting for the Iowa, during the test firing at a new gunnery range in Oregon.

As part of the training they would be spotting for a pair of Cruisers doing shore bombardment training off Saint Nicolas Island.

After The Days Of Infamy

October 3, 1943

Lt. Marks returned to the Iowa on the day before the ship is scheduled to leave the yard. Lt. Price is scheduled to leave the ship before she departs the next morning.

During dinner in the wardroom, Lt. Marks holds court, talking about his experiences with the civilian. "Now this is no shit. The guy was an oil well driller before the war, and had never flown in anything, except that B-25 he flew in on. That plane is like a flying whore house, with carpeting, leather seats, and even a head. The guy's project had enough juice to take it away from an Army Supply General, who had it converted for him and his staff to use exclusively.

"The first day, I got him turnin green within the first five minutes in the air. But he hung on, barfed in his lunch bag, and insisted we go on. He wouldn't talk about his project, but he turned out to be a decent guy."

The Weapons Officer, Commander Mike Phillips, was the same age as Price, and knew part of the modifications to the Fire Control Computer was a change to increase the resolution to the Spotting inputs. He turned to Price and said, "Is that guy part of the project you are doing?"

Price gave him an icy stare and replied, "You gentlemen are pushing the envelope. I suggest you cease this line of discussion completely, or risk finishing the war in Leavenworth. I can't discuss anything about this project, and hope you will take my warning seriously."

The conversation abruptly stopped, and everyone hurried through their dessert before quickly departing.

Price was waiting at the Quarterdeck when the Captain returned from a dinner engagement. They retired to his stateroom, and Price reported the Wardroom speculation, and his warning.

He then told the Captain, "The special ammunition you will load at Seal Beach are shells designed to penetrate Jap island bunkers. The Project is to develop a process to knock them out using offshore 16 inch gunnery. If successful, it can greatly reduce the casualties that taking the bunkers with troops on the ground, have been taking. The firing tests in Oregon will be a dress rehearsal used to evaluate and optimize the process before the Iowa deploys it in the South Pacific early next year."

"Now we both know how scuttlebutt works. By this time tomorrow, everyone on board will know all about the conversations in the wardroom tonight. I must insist that you stop offshore, on your way down to Seal Beach and use the 1MC to broadcast a warning to the entire crew. Tell them that if word of this project leaks out, the Japs could take countermeasures that could defeat our new tactic. After the firing tests are complete, the Iowa will spend Christmas in Seattle."

"However, the Office of Naval Intelligence and the FBI will monitor this ship and crew. If the slightest whiff about the project leaks out, the ship and crew will be quarantined, and spend Christmas anchored at some isolated island in Alaska."

"The source of any leak will be found and that individual can and will be tried for treason."

October 4, 1943

The next morning, Elmer and Wade boarded the B-25, and flew back to DC.

After The Days Of Infamy

October 10, 1943

A larger group of Seebees with newly granted Top Secret Clearances arrive at the Farm. They live in tents near the gate while they build two barracks buildings, a warehouse and a chow hall there.

October 12, 1943

Lt. Price returned to the Iowa at the Hunters Point Shipyard in San Francisco, where he oversees the final main and secondary battery alignments prior to the ship departing for the Channel Island Gunnery Range.

Over the next few weeks, Iowa conducts a wide range of intensive crew training and firing exercises against main battery shore bombardment, anti-ship , and secondary batteries antiaircraft targets.

After dropping Elmer in San Francisco, the B-25 dropped Wade at Coos Bay, where he directed the final preparations at the Firing Range.

November 1, 1943

US Marines land on Bougainville in the Solomon Islands.

November 6, 1943

The Red Army liberates the city of Kiev.

All across the defeated countries of Europe, the unrest builds, and resistance groups form. Even in Italy and Germany, discontent is building.

November 11, 1943

American air power continues to hit Rabaul.

November 14, 1943

Heavy American bombers hit Tarawa, in the Gilbert Islands.

November 22, 1943

Wade and Elmer return to DC and start a final intense study of the completed target models.

November 25, 1943

Americans and Japanese fight the naval Battle of Cape St. George between Buka and New Ireland. Admiral Arleigh Burke's destroyers distinguish themselves.

Rangoon is bombed by American heavy bombers.

December 2, 1943

Wade, Elmer, and Betty depart DC for the West Coast, at 10:00 AM. Shortly after takeoff, Betty closes the curtain between the cabin and flight deck, while Elmer opened a bottle of champagne. Wade poured the drinks while Elmer lowered two of the seats to make a bed.

After sharing drinks, Betty started "getting comfortable". She had not made love with Wade, but Hekoi approached her the day before departure, and told her to please make love with her man.

Betty pulled her sweater over head, turned her back to Wade, and said, "Can you unfasten my bra? Since you will be getting off the plane last, Elmer gets to fuck me first, but

I've been looking forward to you getting in my pants every since Hekoi told me to take good care of you."

Wade removed her bra, flipped it to the table, put both hands on her breasts, kissed her below her right ear, and whispered, "I've been waiting for the opportunity since that first day at the office."

Wade then turned, told Elmer to have a great time, and went up to the flight deck, to leave the couple in peace. Although they had shared a bed and love making with Helen, being alone and intimate together was special. By the time, Wade returned to the cabin, the B-25 was on final to the San Francisco airport.

Once on the ground, Elmer had to wait for the FBI officer to drive him from the airport to Treasure Island, where the ship is berthed. He joined Wade and Betty for a meal and a drink while the B-25 was being serviced and refueled.

They were walking back to the plane, when the FBI guy finally arrived. The man is pissed, because the group was always supposed to have an armed escort. He was just getting wound up when all three pulled out their personal weapons, and told him to shut up.

Elmer rejoined the Iowa in San Francisco, about the same time Wade and Betty finished a passionate lovemaking secession, and were landing in Coos Bay. They checked into a local hotel and shared a room. The next morning, they drove out to the range site, where they would stay at separate floors of the BOQ building.

December 5, 1943

Seebees break ground on a four story building beside the Quonset huts. It will become the Design Center for the

Airship Carrier Development Program.

The top floor of the Design Center will contain offices for the senior staff and two conference rooms.

On the third floor will be an open bay filled with drafting tables, and the second floor will contain more offices, a canteen, a supply room, and, a drawing reproduction and storage center.

A first floor will contain a reception and security center, offices for personal, a nurse, purchasing, and finance.

A deep basement will have a dock for shipping and receiving, a small warehouse, and a huge model and template shop.

December 10, 1943

The Iowa approaches the test range before dawn, and launches both scout planes. Wade is the observer in the plane piloted by Lt. Marks. As the light develops over the target area, the Iowa fires an initial ranging shot, based on the ship's computed position and a set of map coordinates. Wade observes the shell impact, a half mile West, and a mile South of the target. He calls in spotting corrections, and Iowa fires another shell.

It takes a dozen and a half spotting corrections before the shell falls within 50 yards of the target. At this point, Elmer sends a message to end the test.

The Iowa secures from General Quarters, and steams Northwest for four hours, and then South for another three before running in circles until midnight. During the next test, Betty will film the impact zone using a long range camera, from inside an armored blockhouse.

Elmer is in the same blockhouse and is acting as the

Test Controller. Because of the tight security at the range, and his recent promotion to Lt. Cmdr., he is the senior officer at the range site. His ground floor BOQ quarters include a conference room, a private head, and a larger bedroom, which he and Betty put to good use.

The first day's tests are repeated over the next three days. On the third day, the ninth shell falls within 50 yards of the target zone, and Wade's TBS message is, "Commence Final Salvo Operations."

That command releases the full fury of Iowa's main Batteries, and each turret fires five salvos. When the thunder finally stops, the target zone, and the three test wells are obliterated.

Instead of returning to the Iowa, Lt. Marks drops Wade off at the Coos Bay Airport, and the Iowa departs for the Puget Sound. The other VIP BOQ Quarters are also on the ground floor, and Betty joins him there that night.

After a day to let the fumes from the explosives clear, an evaluation team starts to excavation using heavy equipment to determine the degree of destruction the special armor piercing shells did to the three wells.

December 15, 1942

After recovering from his injuries, Lt. Cmdr. Boyd joins Enterprise, promising to write Dorthy every day.

December 16, 1943

The initial assessment of the evaluation team is that the shells did their job, pulverizing the rock in the target area to a depth beyond the fifty feet that had been excavated so far. Their work would continue, but Wade. Elmer, and Betty are ready to return to DC.

A.G. Kimbrough

When Admiral Raymond Spruance returns to the states to spend a Christmas leave with his family, A B-25 is waiting for him on the tarmac when he steps off the plane from Hawaii. A Marine Major hands him a set of orders directing him to fly directly to DC for a meeting with Admiral King, the Chief of Naval Operations.

December 17, 1943

The next morning, Admiral Raymond Spruance is taken to the White House, where he meets with the President, Admiral King, and the Director of Naval Intelligence. He is briefed on the Javelin Project, and his orders to take command of the Task Force from the Yorktown. Because of security issues, only key members of his staff will join him on the Yorktown the day before she departs.

The Admiral is on a plane headed home for Christmas by sundown. His, and his key staff's detailed briefing will take place at sea.

The Iowa docks at the Puget Sound Navy Yard. All hands get generous liberty passes, but no one is granted leave. A Marine Major with a briefcase chained to his wrist, and wearing a forty-five, is waiting at the dock. He is the first one to walk up the gangway to the Quarterdeck. He tells the OOD that he has orders for Captain Baker.

The Major is escorted to the Captain's office, where he unlocks the briefcase, and hands a heavy envelope to Captain Baker. The Major departs after the Captain signs for the envelope.

Captain Baker opens the outer envelope, reads the orders inside, and placed the second envelope inside his personal safe.

After The Days Of Infamy

December 23, 1943

Iowa is moved to the most remote pier, with only one crane, and a railroad spur, where an ammunition train waits. The day is spent unloading enough special armor piercing shells to refill the magazines.

December 26, 1943

USS Enterprise departs North Island Naval Air Station, where her fighter Squadron's planes were replaced with the latest version of the Corsair. One torpedo squadron is also replaced with Corsairs. The Ship heads West for a 100 miles before turning Northwest.

USS Essex Departs Pearl Harbor, also carrying fighter squadrons equipped with new Corsairs. She heads due North.

December 28, 1943

Admiral Spruance arrives at the Alameda Naval Air Station, where Yorktown working parties are loading the last of the Arctic foul weather gear. His arrival is just as unexpected as the Arctic gear, and the OOD scrambles to have the welcoming honors ready.

The dinner conversation at the Farm is subdued, and no one lingered after dessert.

By the time they reach their cottage, Hekoi is sobbing. Wade carried their daughter to her crib. He returned to take her mother in his arms, and kissed the top of his love's head.

She looked up at him and said, "I can't bear the thought of loosing you. Are you sure you have to put yourself in danger?"

A.G. Kimbrough

Wade took her head in both hands and brushed away her tears with his thumbs. I'm terrified of loosing my family, and I have to do this because I'm the only one that can spot those targets. The only way I can protect those I love, is to do everything possible to make this mission a success. If I don't make it back, my family will be well taken care of, and protected."

Hekoi's face turned grim, and her tears stopped. She turned and headed for their bedroom, pulling off her clothes. Wade followed her and started pulling off his shirt.

She finished disrobing, and said, "If this is the last night we make love, I want you to make another baby, so no rubbers."

Helen was also in tears as they entered their bedroom. "I had hoped you were safe from combat with this assignment. I know you have to go, but promise me you will come back."

Elmer also had a few tears, and embraced her. "You know I can't guarantee I'll make it back, but if I don't, you know I will love you always."

December 29, 1943

After enjoying the holiday with family and friends, Wade and Elmer bid them a bittersweet goodbye and board the B-25. They land in Seattle and take the waiting Captain's gig to the Iowa.

The USS Yorktown departs Alameda Naval Station where her fighter Squadron's planes have also been replaced with the latest version of the Corsair. One torpedo squadron was also replaced with Corsairs. The Ship heads West for 100 miles before turning Northwest.

154

After The Days Of Infamy

December 30, 1943

All liberty ended at noon, and another special train drops off three boxcars at the pier. Most of the crew thought they wouldn't unload them until the following day. But, at 2000 hours, an all hands working party is called out. The boxcars are filled with enough arctic foul weather gear for the entire crew as well as the special passengers. They are distributed before midnight, when the Special Sea Detail is set. By 0400, the Iowa is headed out to sea.

December 31, 1943 2345

Captain Baker orders the ship to slow to five knots, and retires to his cabin. He opens the safe and the second envelope. Ten minutes later, he returns to the bridge, and orders a new course heading of 270 degrees at 20 knots.

The scuttlebutt had increased to a firestorm level when the arctic gear came aboard, and everyone was sure they weren't likely to be going to the South Pacific anytime soon.

At Midnight, the message came over the 1MC "All Department Heads, Division Officers, and Division Chiefs report to the Ward Room".

A.G. Kimbrough

Crucible

January 1, 1944 0100:

The Iowa Ward Room was full and missing the usual Stewards. A movie screen is set up on one wall beside a lectern, and the Chief Photographers Mate is manning the movie projector.

"Attention On Deck", rang out as Captain Baker entered. He is followed by Elmer and Wade, who take seats beside the lectern.

Captain Baker walks to the lectern, and says, "Gentlemen, We have received a message from the Commander In Chief." He points at the movie projector and the lights go out.

After a couple of seconds, the screen shows President

Roosevelt in the Oval Office.

"Officers and men of the USS Iowa, tonight I am honored to speak to you about a grave threat to our country, and a large portion of humanity. The Japanese have formed an unholy alliance with the Nazis.

"The Japanese plan to launch an attack on America, using their airship carriers flying over the North pole. Their weapons will be bombs containing nerve gas. Those bombs will explode at 5000 feet, and each one can kill every living thing in a 100 squire mile area. The Nazis will have support ships in the Atlantic to refuel and re-arm the airships.

"After the nerve gas decimates America's major population centers, those same airships will fly on to Germany. The Airships will refuel and re-arm there before devastating the population and industrial centers of the Soviet Union.

"This attack will happen this Spring, unless your mission is successful.

"If your mission is successful, even if we lose this ship and all of you, your sacrifice will save your families and loved ones from a horrible death, and shortened the war.

"The American people will never forget your valor, and I wish you Godspeed.

"Good Night."

The screen darkens, and the lights return.

Captain Baker returned to the lectern and spoke. "This mission, called the Javelin Project, is NOT a suicide mission. It has been planned for two years, and we have critical intelligence from the target area. Our guests, Lt. Commander Price and Mr. Callahan have been spearheading Project Javelin since its inception.

Lt. Commander Price, is the man who shot down the first airship, and Mr. Callahan spent seven years at one of the target sites."

"I'll now turn over the balance of the presentation to them. The days ahead will be busy for all of us, so don't ask questions tonight. We will answer them over the next few days, and the entire crew will see this same presentation.

Price moved to the lectern and went through a rehearsed presentation. Wade replaced the Chief and turned on a slide projector. The first two slides were of the mock-ups of the Helium wells and Processing site, followed by the airship hangers and bomb factory.

When the presentation ended at 0300, the meeting ended.

Meetings continued, morning through night over the next three days, until the entire crew of 2700 men had sat through the presentation, while the ship continued moving West.

January 4, 1944

The First Ukrainian Front of the Red Army enters Poland

January 5, 1944

Progress through the storms in the North Pacific was slow, but the Task Force came together, 1000 miles West of the Washington coast. Seas are too rough for using small craft to bring the commanders on board the Flagship for a face-to-face meeting. So, the necessary coordination is done using short range TBS radios.

Because the participants already had their orders, the

four ships will steam together until they are within 200 miles of the target areas. Since the weather was also too bad to risk launching and recovering planes, the carrier escort Destroyers left the fleet and headed East, because the rough seas would negate any support they might supply.

January 20, 1944

Progress continued to be slow because of the increasing heavy weather, but the storms were also reducing the possibility of detection, because of the low ceiling and strong winds.

Their orders called for the carriers to stay on station, 200 miles North of Hokkaido until the Iowa completes her mission.

Iowa departs at sundown, running at flank speed toward the Northeast end of Hokkaido.

January 20, 1944 0400

Through the night a special heating system distributed hot water to melt the accumulated ice on gun mounts, directors, and other topside equipment. The covers are then removed from both scout planes.

January 20, 1944 0700

An hour before dawn, the engines on both scout planes are run up by the Plane Captains, and the pilots carefully go through the preflight checks.

January 20, 1944 0800

At dawn, the Iowa is thirty miles off the projected coastline, although the haze prevents any sight of the island.

When the surface search radar is turned on, the outline of the island is visible on the PPI Scope, No ships are visible, and to the Southwest, the Cape stands out. From Main Plot, Elmer gives the order to turn on the air search radar. He is relieved that no aircraft are detected. Captain Baker orders the ship to take a station twenty miles south of the Cape and to launch both scout planes.

Wade Callahan breathes a sigh of relief as the scout plane staggers into the air, He had been worried that the catapult would malfunction because of the ice. Both scout planes climb to an altitude of 500 feet, just below the cloud ceiling. They would be vulnerable to ground fire, but he could see the approaching coastline.

Ten minutes later, he sees the Airship Hangers on the horizon. Wade keyed the TBS transmit button. "Target area in sight. Adequate visibility. Fire one ranging shot."

Elmer pressed his transmit key and replied, "Fire one".

The middle gun of Turret One shattered the stillness of the morning. Wade saw the shell plunge through the cloud layer and explode a thousand yards beyond and two thousand yards to the left of the hanger.

"Spot One K over and two K to the left. Fire Second Ranging Shot."

"Roger that, Firing Second Ranging Shot."

On the fifth ranging shot, the High Explosive (HE) shell blew a large hole in the nearest hanger. Wade keyed the transmitter and said, "On Target, All Turrets Free for twelve rounds each gun."

The volleys fell on the target area, and by the time they stopped, the Airship Carrier base was a flaming ruin.

Both scouts made a low pass over the base with their

cameras running.

Wade reported, "Target One destroyed. Stand by for Target Two."

The lead scout plane headed Southwest until the Nerve Bomb Factory was visible. A developing cloud of Ack Ack bursts were also visible ahead of the plane.

January 20, 1944 0841

"Target Two, is ready for first ranging shot."

"Five K over and three K right."

The anti-aircraft shell bursts are coming closer, and Lt. Marks pulls the scout plane up into the clouds and makes a hard turn to the right.

The other scout plane observer is a mile behind, and still under the ceiling. He keyed his transmitter, and said, "Spot one K under and three K right."

The shell bursts soon approach the second scout, and they too are forced into the cloud cover.

January 20, 1944 0910

The Iowa TBS breaks into action, "Radar shows multiple aircraft headed your way."

Lt. Marks replied to Wade, "Better check your guns, I gotta a feeling we're gonna need them."

Wade had never fired the guns, but the crew chief had shown him how to service and operate them. He figured that it couldn't be more difficult than shooting ducks on the wing. Except these ducks could shoot back.

They dropped back below the clouds in time to see the last ranging shot land in the middle of the bomb factory.

"On Target, Fire for effect!"

Several fighters dropped out of the clouds and headed in their direction. Lt. Marks said, "Hang on," dropped a wing and made a tight climbing turn into the clouds. Tracers followed them, from two different directions.

Wade fired, leading the nearest fighter that is trying to keep the scout plane in sight. When Wade's tracers crossed in front of him, the fighter broke off his pursuit and disappeared into the clouds.

January 20, 1944 0930

Both scouts kept dropping out of the clouds checking that the bombardment was still impacting the bomb factory. The fighters headed at them every time the scouts are seen. When the bombardment ceased, both scouts made a quick pass over the target area with their cameras rolling. The factory is in flames, with multiple secondary explosions. When he is back in the clouds, Wade keys the TBS, "Target Two is destroyed, repeat, Targets One and Two both destroyed. We are moving to the next target area.

Admiral Spruance is listening to the TBS and orders all strike aircraft launched. He then ordered the carriers to run South at flank speed.

Both scouts run North until they are over the coast where they run East, following the coastline.

The Iowa is running East at flank speed.

January 20, 1944 0943

The scouts drop out of the clouds, and run South, looking for the railroad tracks that will lead them to Targets Three and Four. When they sight the Helium Processing

Facility, they climb back in the clouds and turn North.

Three minutes later, they drop back down and see the coastline ahead.

January 20, 1944 1013

The scout planes continue to orbit the spot where they flew over the coast until a TBS Message informs them Iowa has the scouts on radar and is located just North of them. Scout Two drops a flare, which is seen by the Iowa.

January 20, 1944 1025

When Iowa announces they are in position, both scouts turn South and approach Target Three. It takes nine ranging shots to ensure that the shells are falling on the well complex. Bombardment had just started when a dozen fighters drop through the clouds. Explosions in the impact zone are lighting up the area and have guided the fighters through the clouds from miles away.

Again, the scouts are forced to seek the safety of the clouds until the bombardment ends. Cameras roll again to record the damage before the scouts turn to run East into the clouds.

Wade reports the destruction of Target Three.

January 20, 1944 1042

The ranging on Target Four begins, but the fighters arrive before the target is being hit. It's necessary for the scouts to bounce into the clouds to escape them.

Finally, a ranging shell hits the center of the Helium Processing plant. It triggers a huge fire when a natural gas storage tank ruptures.

After The Days Of Infamy

January 20, 1944 1053

When the rumble of the bombardment ends, a TBS message from the Iowa warns, "Radar has a large group of planes headed this way. Take your pictures and get out of there. We have boats in the water to pick up you and the film."

Wade replied, "Aye Aye, sir," while Lt. Marks turns the scout back to the North.

Lt. Marks kept the plane at the lower edge of the clouds as they approach, with the second scout trailing two miles behind and a mile to the East.

When they are within a mile of the burning Helium Processing plant, Marks drops to 200 feet, and at a half mile Wade starts the camera rolling, while shooting stills with a 35mm camera. Just as the plane pulls up at the end of the run, three fighters dive through the clouds behind them.

Wade drops the camera and fires his machine guns at the pursuers while Marks twists and turns in a desperate effort to escape. The nearest Zero flies into Wade's tracers and explodes as his shells stitch a pattern across their port wing.

As they reach the relative safety of the clouds, Lt. Marks turns East and asks, "Are you okay Wade?"

"Yes, but we have some holes in the port wing, and it looks like we're loosing fuel."

"Lets go home, but we need to check on Harris before we do."

At that moment, Lt. Harris, the pilot of the second scout keyed his transmitter, "We're going in for a final camera run."

Marks turned South and bounced just below the cloud

layer. They could see the other scout, trailing smoke, with three fighters firing at it. Ten seconds later, the scout exploded.

Lt. Marks pulled up and said "Damn-it, they're gone!"

Wade keyed the transmitter, and said, "Mission Accomplished. Target Four destroyed. We lost Scout Two and are heading home loosing fuel."

The reply came from Elmer. "Well done! Boats are in the water on our starboard side to retrieve you and the film. We expect to be under air attack in five minutes, so be sure you turn on the IFF, and approach from the North. God Speed my friend."

January 20, 1944 1105

The Iowa is firing at the approaching dive bombers with everything but the main batteries. She is also moving North at ten knots. The two Motor Whaleboats are running 500 yards off her starboard beam.

Lt. Marks lines up with the boats, rolls the canopy back, and the scout touches down a hundred yard ahead of them. The sea are rough even though Iowa is putting out an oil slick. As the plane settles on the water, a wingtip catches a wave and flips the plane on its back.

Wade had exchanged his parachute for an inflatable life jacket and the backpack containing the film canisters. He smashed his forehead during the impact, and it stunned him. The cold water revived him and he struggled to escape the cockpit.

Eventually Wade surfaced and started to swim to the wing. Marks helped him climb up on it. The nearest boat was racing toward them when a Zero dropped out of the clouds with its machine guns firing. Wade didn't even have time to go back in the water as the shells stitched across the scout wreckage and continued toward the approaching boat. The boat exploded when the tracers ripped through its fuel tank.

The Zero started a turn toward the second boat when hit by fire from a 40 mm AA battery, and the Zero explodes.

Wade looked for Marks and only found a bloody smear where shell holes made a line across the wing.

January 20, 1944 1115

Wade is shaking uncontrollably by the time the crew pulled him into the other motor whaleboat. As soon as he is laying in the bilge, the boat starts a flank speed chase to catch the twisting and turning battleship.

The first wave of dive bombers scored three direct hits and two near misses. A stairway is lowered to the waterline on the Starboard side, and a pair of big sailors are at the bottom waiting to assist the boat crew boarding. Wade is hustled to the bow. The crew orders require him to be first to board the stairs. One crewmen attempts to take the backpack, and Wade refuses to surrender it.

He is grabbed by the sailors on the stair landing and hurried up to the main deck where two more guys pull him to the nearest hatch. As he steps through the hatch, a bomb explodes on the mount 53 barbette and its magazine exploded. The blast knocked him into the passageway, and down a ladder to the lower deck.

Dazed, unknown hands guide him through smoke filled passageways and to the nearest aid station. Wade sees Elmer waiting there to take the backpack. He attempts to speak, and then everything goes black.

A.G. Kimbrough

January 23, 1944.

When Wade opens his eyes, Elmer is seated at the desk in their shared stateroom. When he coughed, Elmer walked over and asked, "Do you want some water?"

"That would be good. How long have I been out?"

Elmer looked grim, and said, "It's been three days. I thought for a while, we might lose you."

Wade questions, "Why aren't I in Sick Bay, if I was in that condition?"

Elmer replied, "Because it's overflowing with guys, that are a whole lot worse off than you."

Wade groaned, and asked, "It was that bad?"

"We took six direct hits, including one on the flag bridge and another down the forward stack. It didn't break her back, but it came close to sinking us. The ceramic armor probably saved us. Those armor-piercing bombs that hit those plates broke them up, but didn't go through them.

"Those attacks disabled or killed over half the crew. If the fighters from our carriers hadn't arrived when they did, the last group of bombers would have sunk us. Now, drink a little water, lay back, and relax. The doc said to keep you horizontal for another twenty-four hours. I'll get someone to stay with you while I'm on deck. We're going to launch the balloon transmitter, and I have to shoot some pictures for Betty."

Wade questioned, "I though they had two Photographers Mates assigned to take pictures for her?"

"They were on the Flag Bridge when it was hit. It killed everyone on that level. At least it didn't penetrate through the deck armor into the Main Bridge. Now go back to sleep. This message is too important to rely on some deck ape to

168

get it off."

Because of the storm, the outside main deck is off limits, and the Starboard inside passageway is blocked by the wreckage from the explosion of Mount 53. Elmer made his way aft before climbing up to the 02 level and stepping outside, above turret three. Below him, a pair of sailors fought to attach a package to a cluster of three Helium filled weather balloons. By the time it's ready to release, Elmer has shot half a roll of film.

In less than a minute, the balloons disappears into the clouds. The package contains a battery powered transmitter, which will send Dit Dit Dit Daw (V), when it reaches 5000 feet. It will keep transmitting until the battery run down.

Lt. Commander Boyd gets two more kills defending the Iowa. and flies his shot-up Corsair back to the Enterprise. He has shell fragments in both legs and severe frostbite.

A.G. Kimbrough

Homecoming

January 24, 1944 0200

The recommissioned USS Walker,is a four stack destroyer from the Reserve Fleet. Walker is upgraded with radar, and on radar picket duty 200 miles West of Washington's Coast. The last refueling tanker had passed over a package of sealed orders along with the regular containers of movies and mail.

New orders direct her to maintain a full-time monitor on a specific radio frequency. They must re-transmit anything received on the channel over the Alert channel.

Third class Radioman Schultz had music from a mainland radio station on a speaker, just loud enough to hear above the background static from the special channel.

When the signal broke over the static, "Dit Dit Dit

A.G. Kimbrough

Daw," it repeated every thirty seconds. Before it repeated for the fourth time, the Radioman was sending over the Alert Channel "Special Message received, Letter Vee, in Morse Code, every thirty seconds."

January 24, 1944, 0543:

The White House Communications Center receives the message. The Naval Officer on duty takes it up to the residence to wake the President.

Roosevelt had only been asleep for three hours, and the strain of events is wearing him down. Eleanor attempts to get him to return to bed. It energized him, and he didn't return before spending two hours on the phone, and sending several messages.

January 24, 1944, 0800:

The message is waiting when the Project Team arrive at the Office. Waiting for news has been hard on everyone, and the cryptic V message only indicates they have destroyed the targets. There is no indication of the cost.

January 27, 1944

After Admiral Spruance transfers from the Enterprise to the Iowa, the Carriers turn South to resupply and refuel before returning to Hawaii.

January 28, 1944

The Russian Army completes encirclement of two German Army corps at the Koraun Pocket, south of Kiev.

After The Days Of Infamy

February 18, 1944, 2300:

The Iowa limps into the Puget Sound Navy Yard and goes directly to Drydock Two. A line of ambulances is waiting on the dock. Betty is also there, waiting to board. Even though it is too dark for pictures, she can see the horrific damage.

Finally, after the wounded are off the ship, she follows the Shipyard Commander, and Director Kelly to the bridge. Her heart skips a beat when she catches sight of Elmer and Wade, who has a bandage on his head. All three have a hard time avoiding showing the emotions they feel.

Captain Baker gives the butcher's bill, with 657 KIA and 786 wounded on the Iowa. The ship suffered major damage, and will be in the shipyard a long time.

Admiral Spruance reported 38 fighter pilots KIA and thirteen wounded from the three carriers. Those losses would have much higher, except that Admiral Spruance ordered the carriers to turn on searchlights to guide the fighters back to safe landings, through the clouds. The carriers are in route to Hawaii.

February 19, 1944, 0830:

After the breakfast meeting breaks up, Betty, Wade, Elmer, Captain Baker and Admiral Spruance take a boat ride over to Seattle, and board the B-25 for a flight to DC. They are all glad to be on a plane with reclining and comfortable seating which allows them to sleep during the flight.

February 19, 1944, 1640:

The meeting with Roosevelt lasts until dinner time when everyone is dismissed and directed to return the next morning to help prepare for a Presidential address to Congress and the nation. The reunions at the Farm are joyful, and no one gets much sleep.

February 27, 1944

The Design Center is completed, and the new support staffing is in place. Those people are all cleared for Top Secret and live off base.

When Lt. Boyd reaches the San Diego Naval Hospital, Dorthy is overjoyed to be reunited, even if he had to become a patent again

March 1, 1944, 2030:

The great hall went silent when Roosevelt enters. For the first time he does not hide his wheelchair.

Roosevelt struggles to stand behind the podium, and speaks, "My fellow Americans, tonight I will speak to you without pretense or any thought of politics. When we discovered the nature of the Airship Carrier threat in the Spring of 42, the Office of Naval Intelligence formed a team to develop countermeasures to it.

"In April of 42, an American and his Japanese wife escaped Japan by sailing across the Northern Pacific. After hearing about the Airship Carriers, they brought us vital intelligence about the Helium wells location.

"That man is a vital member of the Project Javelin team. Because Helium is not flammable, the Japanese Airship Carriers cannot be destroyed by fighter planes firing tracers, unlike the Zeppelins in World War One, which used Hydrogen for lifting gas.

"Destruction of the Helium wells would force the

After The Days Of Infamy

Airship Carriers to rely on a more flammable lifting gas, and become very vulnerable to tracer bullets.

"The Project Javelin team developed a plan to send a new generation fast Battleship across the Northern Pacific, in mid-winter, using the clouds from arctic storms to hide from detection. The mighty 16 inch guns could then destroy the Helium wells from offshore.

"In July of last year, intelligence assets in Germany and Japan provided a warning of an impending attack that could kill most of our population, plus half of the civilized world's population.

"This diabolical plot, called the Ultimate Solution, would use the Japanese Airship Carrier Fleet to fly over the North Pole and bomb our industrial and population centers with nerve gas bombs.

"Each bomb would explode at 5000 feet altitude and the sinking nerve gas from each bomb, would kill every living thing for a hundred square miles. After dropping their bombs, the Airship Carrier Fleet would fly out into the Atlantic. They would meet waiting German support ships which would refuel them before they flew on to Germany.

"In Germany, they would refuel and rearm with German made nerve gas bombs, before attacking the Population and Industrial Centers in the Soviet Union.

"Following the nerve gas decimation of the Soviet Union's population, the Airship Carrier Fleet would return to Japan.

"Our Japanese intelligence assets alerted us to the details of the planned Ultimate Solution, including the location of the Airship Base and the nerve gas Bomb factory, both on the Northeast tip of Hokkaido Island, thirty miles West of the Helium wells.

"With no other choice, the Team had to expand the scope of Project Javelin to include the bombardment of the Airship base and the nerve gas Bomb factory. There was only one fast Battleship available.

"The USS Iowa, would have to bombard both areas. The doubling of the missions significantly increased the likelihood she would face heavy aircraft attacks before she could escape into the arctic weather.

"Because of the danger, we could not risk having our carriers provide close support, since they represent much of our fleet carrier assets in the Pacific. The final decision to approve the mission was mine, and I took it knowing it could condemn the crew of the Iowa.

"Thirty-five days ago, I received the cryptic message that the targets were destroyed. The Iowa returned to port ten days ago. She is twisted, broken, and burned, and the cost was too high, but she fulfilled her mission, and the threat from a nerve gas attack is postponed.

"Because Germany was an instigator and willing participant in this plot, I'm asking the Congress to declare a state of war exists between the United States of America, and Germany and her Allies.

"I also urge our Allies in the conflict with Japan to join us in a state of war against Germany. Tomorrow, I will start actions to provide large scale material and military support to the Soviet Union, and any other nation seeking to throw of the yoke of Nazi domination."

An Expanded War

March 4, 1944

With the destruction of the Japanese airship carriers, Hitler orders full production of the latest generation V4 rockets, configured with nerve gas warheads and field mobile launchers.

He also orders development of a submarine based launcher for the same weapon.

March 5,1944

When Rio started to create the propaganda scripts for broadcasts to Japan, he struggled for hours to put his thoughts in a persuasive format. Betty realized that Rio needed help, and tracked down Toshie at an internment camp, where she was publishing the camp newspaper. Betty pulled the right government strings and Toshie arrived at the Farm a week later.

Toshie could have slept in the luxurious B-25 during the evening flight from Burbank to DC, but she was too excited. A Navy car picked her up at the camp in the high California desert and drove her to the Burbank Airport. Two Navy Captains were the other passengers, and neither spoke to her.

The ride from DC to the farm was going against the morning rush hour traffic. Betty was waiting for her at the gate, and the car took them to Betty's cottage, where Toshie would stay until her quarters were ready.

Betty insisted Toshie relax until the early afternoon, and left her in the cottage, to attend a meeting, saying she would pick her up for lunch around 1:00 PM.

Because of threats from some who had objected to her LA Times article, Toshie used a different name at the camp, and her family were at a different camp in Northern California,. She kept to herself in the unmarried woman's barracks and made no friends there.

After Betty returned to her Quonset hut office, Toshie unpacked her suitcase and hung her clothes in a new wardrobe Betty had waiting for her. Tired, she lay down on the couch and slept.

Betty returned at 1:00 and took Toshie over to a Quonset hut with a small canteen. After enjoying a ham sandwich and Southern style ice tea (new to her), the ladies went next door. The Quonset hut, formerly the model shop is now a recording and film studio. It also has a conference room and three offices.

Betty pointed to the door across from the conference room, and the window had her name printed on it. Toshie opened the door, and saw a large metal desk with a Royal typewriter, a telephone, a reference table, file cabinet, bookshelf, and a mimeograph machine. Even at the LA Times, Toshie had only a small desk, with a shared portable typewriter and telephone. The office made a strong positive impression on her.

Betty knocked at the door labeled Rio Watanabe, and a middle aged Japanese man answered. He had thinning hair, a big smile, and gave Betty a big hug. You really did it! This young lady will rescue me from the perils of publication.

After hallway introductions, the three went to the conference room, and spent two hours going over the basics of a planned series of broadcasts meant to further destabilize the Japanese government's hold over the population. A planned series of B29 missions would drop thousands of crystal radios over population centers. High powered radio transmitter equipped B29s would make regular nightly broadcasts of propaganda programs. Rio and Toshie are responsible for producing a series titled "A Common Sense End Of The War."

Betty excused herself to make a few necessary telephone calls. Rio took Toshie into his office and started to review his ideas for the first script.

Toshie had declined her parents attempts at an arranged marriage, and while at the Times, she was too busy to become serious about anyone. Her few dates were not productive. All most guys wanted was to get in her pants. Even though she considered herself a modern girl, her long-term goal was to have a husband and children.

After being fired from the LA Times, she became an untouchable in the LA Japanese community. Not everyone disagreed with her position, but the social pressure exerted by those who did, was immense.

She watched Rio closely as he talked. Not only was he

self assured, but she thought he was cute.

Rio is aware of her gaze, and he feels a magnetism developing between them.

At 5:00 PM Betty returned, and they all walked across the park to the row of cottages. Toshie noticed that Rio's cottage was next door to Betty's.

Betty unlocked her door, and said, "We will have dinner at the big house at 7:00. The key people eat there most evenings. The chef is a master, and it will be a good opportunity for you to meet them. You have time for another nap or a bubble bath. I'll be at Rio's place for a drink and some whoopee. I'll shower there afterward."

Toshie is astounded by Betty's casual remark about having sex with Rio. After a long bubble bath, she lay naked on the couch feeling a little jealous. Unable to sleep, she got up at 6:30 and dressed.

At 6:45 Betty returned, wearing a robe and carrying her clothes. She walked over to the bathroom, tossed her clothes in the hamper, hung the robe on a hook, and turned her naked body back to face Toshie.

Noticing Toshie's shocked expression, Betty said, "I'm sorry, I should have said something. Rio and I are in a non-monogamous relationship. Since I'm a very sexual person, who enjoys sex with both men and women, I had to refuse to accept his proposal to be his wife, because I can't have children. I knew I would always be sexually attracted to others. I love Rio and would never do anything to hurt him. We are just lovers, with no strings attached, and I won't have sex with someone in a relationship, unless their partner gives both of us prior permission. The couple who own the big house, Helen and Elmer Price, have what they call, an open marriage, and I have enjoyed sex with both.

After The Days Of Infamy

"If I made you uncomfortable, I'm sorry. If you wish, I'll stay over at Rio's place until your quarters are ready. I thought living with me until your cottage is finished would give you a chance to get to know everyone. The group here is pretty nonjudgmental. We even skinny-dip in the pool every Friday night."

Toshie replied, No, no, I don't mind. I guess I've led a very sheltered life. I don't mind nudity, or non-monogamous relationships, but I think I'll skip the Friday night skinny dips."

Betty gasped, "Oh my gosh, you're a virgin?"

Toshie did not reply, and just flushed.

Betty said nothing more, and started dressing.

Dinner that night was enjoyable. Toshie found Elmer and Helen Price, the owners of the farm, to be a warm and a delightful couple. Wade Callahan's wife Hekoi, was from Japan and her age. Toshie was sure they would become close friends.

Mickey Imazumi was Rio's best friend, and the man who led the team who designed the Japanese Airship Carriers. He met his wife Gurti, while he was in Germany, learning how to build Zeppelins. Gurti is Heinrich Lehman's younger sister. Heinrich went to UCLA with Rio and Mickey, and his wife Maria was born in Spain.

Everyone made Toshie feel welcome. She knew she would be restricted to the Farm for the duration, both for security, and her own safety. That prospect now seemed less daunting. Seated between Rio and Betty, Toshie is very aware of his proximity.

Over the rest of the week, Toshie and Rio work to refine the first broadcast script. Rio insists that she be the one to

181

narrate the final recording. The mutual attraction continues to grow.

Rio had spoken with Betty, who was aware of the mutual attraction. She insisted there was no problem, as far as she is concerned, with Rio having a relationship with Toshie. Betty, mentioned that Toshie is very shy, and probably is still a virgin.

Toshie continued to avoid any outward sign she was falling in love with Rio. Determined to have a monogamous relationship with a husband and children, she is also unwilling to come between Betty and Rio.

March 7, 1944

Lt. Commander Boyd is discharged from the hospital, promoted to Commander, and receives orders to the Naval Air Station, Patuxent River. The orders call for him to head an evaluation of fighter aircraft for the airship program. He noticed his orders said his Commanding Officer was a Commander Price. He wondered if it could be the Elmer Price from the USS Fletcher, but Price wasn't an aviator.

Expecting the assignment to give at least a year of shore duty, he asks Dorthy to marry him and join him in Virginia. She accepts, but wants to give a month's notice to the Hospital. This delay will give Boyd time to get settled and find them a place to live before she arrives.

Lt. Commander Wycliff receives a promotion to Commander, and orders to report to an engineering facility, just South of DC, in Virginia. The orders don't define his duties, his commanding officer, or even the facility address. They only give him a phone number to call when he arrives at the DC airport.

After The Days Of Infamy

March 11, 1944

Commander Wycliff doesn't understand what his new assignment will be. He has assumed that the Navy will keep him stuck in blimps for the rest of the war and is surprised at the promotion that came with the orders. He carries his bag into the terminal, calls the number. and is told he will be picked up in front of baggage claim within a half hour. A car picks him up at the airport 20 minutes later, and drives into the country South of Fairfax, Virginia. The intense security at the facility gate, and no facility signs are unexpected. The driver drops him off at the entrance of a new looking, four story building. A marine took his bag and footlocker and said they would be in his quarters when he reached them. Another Marine escorts him to a conference room on the fourth floor.

There were five men seated on one side of a large table which has a twenty foot long, cutaway model of an airship carrier. Commander Wycliff at first thinks it must be a model of a Japanese airship carrier. But, then he notices it has stars on the tails. His heart skips a beat, and he realizes that his assignment will make him a part of the team developing the US Airship Carriers.

Commander Elmer Price is known throughout the Navy as the man who shot down the first Japanese Airship Carrier. He introduced himself, "Good afternoon. I'm Elmer Price, an Assistant Director Of Naval Intelligence, and the head of Project Javelin Team. These gentlemen are the key members of the Project team. Because of the mix of civilian and military, we will use first names when we are in an informal setting.

Price then introduced a civilian, seated to his right. "This is Wade Callahan, the Project Javelin Project Manager."

A.G. Kimbrough

Seated next to Callahan is a middle aged Japanese civilian. Price said, "This is Mickey Imazumi, the man who led the team who designed the Japanese Airship Carriers. His defection helped prevent the nerve gas murder, of a large part of the US and Russian populations."

Seated next to Mickey was another civilian. Price said, "Heinrich Lehman is the man who helped design the German Airship Carriers, and stole the Hindenburg, to enable Mickey, his wife, and another important Japanese man, to escape with the critical information necessary to prevent the nerve gas attack.

Seated on Price's left was a man Wycliff recognized from the news reels, as Howard Hughes. Price said, Howard has been the driving force behind the approval of the US Airship Carrier program. Howard is in charge of the Airship Manufacturing process.

Price then said, "Commander Jason Wycliff, is a man who was the fighter squadron Commander of the Airship Carrier Macon.

"He is joining the Javelin Project Team as the Prospective Commanding Officer of Lexington, the first, next generation US Navy Airship Carrier."

Wycliff replied, "Thank you for the greatest opportunity of my career. I'm so pleased to be working with you. Please call me JJ, like all my friends do."

When the meeting ended, Price walked with Wycliff across a grassy area they called the park, to a row of cottages. Price handed him a key and pointed to one, and said, "That one is yours. We meet for dinner at the big house at 1900, where you'll meet the rest of the key team members and their wives."

The food at the dinner was great, the conversations

184

interesting, and Wycliff was given a warm welcome by everyone, particularly an unattached lady named Betty Laurence.

Betty is intrigued by this tall man with a touch of gray at his temples.

March 12, 1944

Commander Boyd thought his assignment would be to evaluate the latest generation of the Corsair. What he discovered, when he met with his new boss, Commander Elmer Price, amounted to Naval Air heresy.

He had been flying the latest generation Corsairs, but his project assignment is to prove that the Army Air Corps P51 Mustang would not be a better choice for airship operations, than the Corsair.

Boyd loved the Corsair, but he quickly learned that the Mustang was a lighter and smaller airplane, since it was not designed to withstand the rigors of hard landings on a carrier flight deck.

The US Airship Carrier design team was fighting space and weight issues because the wood structure would be heavier than the bamboo used by the Japanese Airship Carriers. If the Mustang is acceptable, the weight and size savings will allow the Airship Carrier to carry ten more fighters.

Boyd recalled a story about the Royal Navy's attempt to adapt the Spitfire for carrier operations. The first hard landing resulted in the Spitfire's tail breaking off.

Skeptical at first, He soon learned the Mustang has a longer range, a faster top speed, and it can fly higher. There also were over a hundred of the latest model available. He soon finds the Mustang has better ground handling manners and much better cockpit visibility.

After his third flight, Commander Boyd made up his mind, and starts writing a final report. When he called Commander Price, to inform him the report is ready for review, Price told him to have several copies of the report ready to take with him first thing the next morning.

March 15, 1944

Deiter Fousal is a 28 year-old master mechanic, working as a final assembler in the main V-4 assembly line, located in an underground factory. His girlfriend's family is Jewish, and they were recently taken to a concentration camp.

Deiter had never been political, choosing to use his mechanical skills instead of military service. He wrongly assumed that the actions of the Nazi government would never effect him, or those he loved.

Recognizing he is powerless to save those he loves, he vows revenge.

He uses a tubing cutter to score two tubes on the main engine. The scoring is covered by the connector fittings on the LOX and Alcohol engine connections.

While the scoring will still allow the tubing to pass the Quality Control Pressure Tests, he believes the tubes will fracture as the engine vibrates during flight.

The first engine he sabotages is the last in the first production run of eight. He resolves to score the tubes of every third engine he assembles until he is caught or until the war ends.

After The Days Of Infamy

March 16, 1944

Commander Boyd had just finished his second cup of coffee when a call from reception informs him, his car is waiting at the front entrance. He closes and locks the brief case containing twelve copies of his report, walks out the door, and gets into the waiting Ford. It is driven by a middle aged civilian who appears to have a gun in a shoulder holster. Commander Boyd assumed they are going to Commander Price's office in DC, but the closed mouth driver turned West.

The driver left Boyd at the entrance of a four story building, and a Marine takes him to a fourth floor conference room. By the end of the day he has met the Project team, and received orders to report to the Farm, as the Prospective Carrier Air Group Commander of the Lexington.

After the meeting ended, Price walks with Boyd across the park, and left him the key to the last cottage in a row of cottages. Boyd found the contents of his room at the Naval Air Station Patuxent River BOQ were there. The cottage was nicer than the BOQ, and he thought Dorthy would find it acceptable.

Dinner at the Big House included Farm grown beef and vegetables cooked to perfection. He is given a warm welcome by the other senior people and their wives.

April 10, 1944

The Army Air Corps locates the Eighth Air Force Headquarters in Alexandria Egypt and starts B17 Heavy Bomber operations against German targets from Remote Bases in Northern Africa, the Soviet Union, and Scotland.

April 15, 1944

Dorthy arrives and the ladies at the farm quickly scuttle his plans to sneak off to a Justice of the Peace and get married.

The pending nuptials cause ripples in the community. Rio is in love with Toshie, but keeps his feelings to himself, because their partnership in the broadcasts is working so well.

When Betty mentioned that she is planning to get in Boyd's pants after the reception, Rio confessed his deep feelings for Toshie.

Betty responds, "I believe she's hot for you, but she's an old-fashioned girl who wants a faithful husband and kids. I like that girl a lot, so unless you're willing to give her a ring, back off, because I don't want to see her hurt. You know I don't have any strings on you, and I'm willing to be just friends, without the benefits. There are lots of fish in the sea to satisfy my sex drive. Who knows, after Toshie has a couple of kids she may be ready to explore her options.

The next day Rio hands Elmer a roll of bills and asks him to buy a nice wedding ring.

Toshie was also too aware of the upcoming wedding. As the day approached, she becomes more depressed at her present condition.

April 18, 1944

Michael and Dorothy Boyd are married by a Judge friend of the Price family in the rose garden behind the Big House. Elmer Price is Best Man and Helen, Toshie and Maria are Bridesmaids. The Callahan kids are the Ring-Bearer and Flower Girl.

After The Days Of Infamy

Toshie is shocked to be the one who catches the brides bouquet.

Betty filmed the entire ceremony, in addition to taking many still photos.

The Reception in the Big House is a smashing success, and will be long remembered. Everyone drinks too much, especially Toshie. When she shows signs of too much alcohol, Rio takes her arm, and walks her back to her cottage.

The walk sobered her up enough to throw caution to the wind. When Rio turned to leave after she is safely inside, Toshie put her arms around his neck and gives him a deep, long kiss. Then she steps back with a look of determination on her face, she said, "I can't fight it any more. I love you and want to make love now."

Before Rio can react, Toshie unzips the full length zipper on the side of her dress and starts to step out of it. When she lifts her leg, and loses balance, Rio has to grab her arm to keep her from falling. Then she is in his arms, wearing only a bra and panties.

Rio carries her to the bedroom, gives her kiss on the forehead, and says, "I love you too. If you still feel this way in the morning, when you're sober, I want you to be my wife, in a monogamous, lifetime relationship."

As the party starts breaking up, Betty turned to JJ and said, "Can you help me carry my stuff over to the studio. It's dark, and I would hate to stumble and drop a camera."

JJ smiled and said, 'I'll be happy to help."

They walk across the park to the Quonset hut with her arm in his. Their conversation during the walk features speculation on what Rio and Toshie were doing.

JJ commented, "Toshie has been making moon eyes at Rio all night."

Betty replied," Rio is stuck on her, but she only wants a ring and kids.

After dropping off the camera equipment, the couple start back across the park, her arm back in his.

JJ asked, "I thought you and Rio were together?"

Betty answered, "It's just friends with benefits, and no strings. I can make love with anyone I want, and tonight, I want you."

JJ pulled her closer and said, "That sounds like a fine way to end a great evening."

The newlywed couple escapes the Farm, to spend their weekend honeymoon in a suite at the Willard hotel in DC. The duration is limited by the intense pressure to release the designs for the Lexington.

April 19, 1944

When Toshie wakes at 9:30 the next morning, she has the worst hangover of her life. The previous night's memories are vague. She makes some tea, and after the first sip, she remembers.

Embarrassed at what she considered, her wanton behavior, she blushed, and then remembered Rio's response.

After finishing the tea and a piece of toast, she knew it is late. Unable to face him yet, she runs a bubble bath, and lay there soaking and thinking. The water is cooling when there's a knock at the door.

Toshie grabbed her robe and cracked the door to see

After The Days Of Infamy

Rio.

He steps back and said, "Sorry, I didn't mean to disturb you, but, when you didn't show by 11:00, I got worried. Are you all right?"

"Yes, I'm still a little hung over, but it's getting better."

Toshie opened the door and said, "Please come in, I'm sorry to have put you in an awkward position last night. I had way too much to drink."

Rio stepped inside and pushed the door closed, before saying, "Did you mean what you said? I did."

After a long pause, tears appeared in Toshie's eyes, and she said, "Yes."

The robe drops to the floor, and she stands there, naked.

Rio drops to one knee, opens a small velvet box, and says, "Can I put this on?"

"Oh yes, but you need to be naked first."

He complies with her request, puts the ring on her finger, and carries her into the bedroom.

They didn't return to the office that day.

April 25, 1944

The same Judge married Rio and Toshie in a low key ceremony, followed by a smaller reception. They couldn't leave the Farm and spent their three-day honeymoon in Toshie's cottage.

Everyone in the Javelin Team is working sixteen-hour days, seven days a week. Beside the airship design, the design team is producing the construction blueprints for the Airship Carrier Assembly Building. This massive structure will have four foot thick, steel reinforced brick walls that are 500 feet apart, and 2500 feet long. The 300 feet tall walls will be spanned with a domed wooden structure similar to the airship hull and covered with the same outer skin planned for the airships.

Although the structure will abut one side of the existing furniture factory building, the opposite end of the Assembly Building will have a pair of curved wooden doors which will roll on steel rails to open and close.

Unlike the Army Air Corps, the Navy has an unlimited priority to commission the first Airship Carrier by early 1945, and another every three months thereafter.

Gurti and Hekoi are both pregnant and Helen is running logistics at the Farm.

April 30,1944

The first group of eight mobile V4 launchers are deployed just behind the German front lines. The forces there will be the tip of the spear to slash through the remaining Soviet forces after the devastating series of nerve gas strikes. Two of the nerve gas warheads explode over Moscow, killing Stalin, most of the general staff and the government bureaucracy.

Other warheads target primary airfields, major industrial sites, and the four largest Soviet troop concentrations.

Because of the importance of this operation, Hitler insisted that Walter Dornberger, all the key program staff, including Wernher von Braun, be at the launch site to prevent anything from going wrong.

The last V4 launch countdown proceeds normally, and the rocket lifts off. At 8000 feet, the engine vibrations fracture the weakened LOX and Alcohol connections. When they break loose, the rear of the rocket explodes. Because the forward section of the rocket remains intact, it slows before starting to fall. When it falls to 5000 feet, the warhead explodes, and the crew at the launch site watch in terror, with the knowledge they will soon be dead.

After the cloud of nerve gas not only kills the entire launch crew and the important observers, the 900,000 men at the tip of the spear also are dead, within the next 24 hours.

The German's Russian Campaigns is stalled. nerve gas contamination is longer lasting than predicted and losing all the key engineering talent has stopped V4 production.

Marshal Zhukov, would have been killed by the V4 that exploded above the launch site. He assumes the role of Supreme Military Commander, and begins the long struggle to pull the government, industry, and the military back together.

The German military losses from nerve gas exposure exceed a million men, and the Government can't keep that fact hidden from the public, as the telegrams to their next of kin start to arrive.

May 10, 1944

Oberleutnant Ernst Baldus receives a telegram confirming that his younger brother is missing in action and is presumed dead. He was commanding the crew of a V4 launcher.

The news was not a surprise, since the news of the disaster had spread through his command. Baldus is the exec on U1701, originally a freighter sub, and now the first of 10 Rocket U-boats. A watertight hanger that will contain a pair of V4 launchers has been mounted on the main deck, just forward of the conning tower.

His enthusiasm for the war had faded. He excelled in his previous three combat cruises, and is scheduled to become the Captain of U 1711 as soon as it is commissioned. His present Rocket U-boat is due to leave the yard soon for a test firing in the Eastern Baltic. A successful launch will release the conversion of the remaining nine ships in the class. Their ultimate destiny would be to unleash V4 rockets carrying nerve gas, on the coastal cities of North America.

Disturbed by the death of his last family member, Ernst leaves the boat to spend the night before departure, with his girlfriend, Anna Fischer. She lives with her father, a fisherman, a few miles North of the shipyard. Her father didn't approve of them sleeping together, but didn't forbid it, since they were engaged to be married as soon as he is made a Captain.

Anna knew something was wrong when Ernst arrived. During the night he expressed his dissatisfaction with the prospect of killing millions with the nerve gas rockets. The situation seemed to have no end in sight.

When they went to Anna's room, she insisted that he try to make her pregnant.

May 26, 1944

When U1701 returned from the successful test launches, the shipyard had signs of fresh bombing damage. After heavy bombing attacks by British Lancasters in 1941, all U-boat construction was moved to the a new underground pen which again proved impregnable when B-17's made the two recent attacks on the yard from an unknown location.

After The Days Of Infamy

The U1701 entered the same pen, and sailed past the other nine freighter subs that will be converted to Rocket U boats. At the far end of the subterranean tunnel is the dock for reloading and refueling the V4s, and the sub stops there. Ernst stayed aboard for the next two days and nights overseeing the loading of the next two V4s which contain live nerve gas warheads. Those rockets are due to be fired into Russia.

The LOX and Alcohol fuel will be loaded into the sub's storage tanks on the next day. Baldus makes a last minute inspection of the hanger with the V4s on their launcher, and the hold containing the storage tanks. He also takes a roll of 35 mm film of everything.

With the roll of exposed film hidden in his cap, Ernst departs the base and rides a bus to Anna's house overlooking the fishing boat docks. She has fixed a dinner for the two of them, and her father has gone out.

Anna observes that her lover is subdued during the meal. After the dishes are cleared, he finally opens up.

"This world has gone mad, and I have to take action. I need you to do something for me if you love me."

"Of course, I love you, and will do anything you ask."

Ernst removes the film can from his cap, and says, "I know your father sometimes trades with the English fishing boats. I also know they pay money for information. I need you to get on board an English boat and go to England. When you are there, get in touch with the Americans and tell them everything I told you about the Rocket U-boats, and what the Germans plan to do with them. Don't tell them everything, until you are sure you are talking to the American Intelligence people. Take the this film all the way to America if you can."

The color drained from Anna's face as he spoke.

"That sounds like you want me to commit treason".

His respond is heated, "What Hitler is doing to our country, and the civilized world is the treason. I have to do everything I can do to prevent it."

Anna questioned, "Then why don't you go to England with me? Surely you can provide much more information then I ever could. And we can be together."

Ernst's expression grew serious, and he said, There's something I have to do tomorrow, and if I was missing, every boat in the harbor would be searched."

Her tears started to fall, and she said, "You know I'll do what you ask, but is this the last time I'll see you?"

Ernst kissed away her tears, and said, "It may take time, but I'll find you wherever you are, and then we'll never be apart again."

Anna wanted to believe him, and the couple spent most of the night making sometimes frantic love.

<u>Epilogue</u>

May 29, 1944

The couple parted at dawn, and he returned to the shipyard, while she went down to her father's fishing boat.

She had the coffee ready when he came aboard, and soon overrode his objections, by threatening to go out to sea with a known smuggler that her father hated.

The fishing boat sailed out of the harbor with the rest of the fishing fleet, and were out of sight when the smoke trail rose from the shipyard.

May 31, 1944

When the English fishing boat came out of the fog, it did not respond to her father's hails, or the blue masthead light indicating they had something to trade. Anna came out of the cabin, stood on the bow, and pulled up her sweater to reveal her bare breasts. The English boat changed course and came along side. Her father knew the Captain, and had traded for smuggled goods with him in the past.

A few minutes discussion produced an agreement to

take Anna to their home port in exchange for some trade items that included her father's nearly new Grundig radio. When he embraced Anna goodbye, he placed a small automatic pistol in her pocket. Both he and Ernst had already given her all the cash they had.

The boats parted and continued fishing on the Dogger bank.

During the two day trip back to their home port, a crewman attempted to join her in her bunk. Although she had no English, the automatic gave him a clear message.

June 5, 1944

Anna spent the afternoon in the custody of a British Naval officer, whose German was no better than Anna's English. He left when the young American arrived. Johann Friedman was a second generation German American, whose Jewish Grandparents fled Germany during the First World War. He was tall, blond, a Harvard Graduate, and one of Bill Donovan's OSS European Operators. His German was excellent, and he took her to a safe house in London. During the long drive Anna explained her need to bring critical information about a planned German rocket attacks on the American coastal cities. When he attempted to probe for more details, she said that her source told her to be sure she was talking to an American senior enough to use the information. Johann backed off and did not attempt to pressure her.

They stopped for a nice dinner, before he dropped her off at a safe house, where she had her own bedroom and private bath. Two non German speaking men were there to provide security, and Johann said he would return in the morning with some answers.

The message traffic with DC was heavy all night, with Donovan making the decision to have Johann bring Anna to DC immediately. '

The next day Johann picked up Anna for breakfast and then they boarded a train for Scotland.

After a long train ride they were met by a RAF car and taken to to a remote airbase. A B17 was waiting inside a hanger.

As they boarded the aircraft, Johann explained that the presence of a US aircraft in England violated the 1941 Peace Treaty with Germany.

After they were strapped in, the hanger doors opened, the engines were started, and the plane took off into the darkness. The flight to Newfoundland was long and uncomfortable, with neither of the passengers getting much sleep.

Back in Washington the Navy was insisting that because the threat was Naval based, the Navy must have the lead in interrogating and evaluating this intelligence source. The OSS was insisting that since they recovered the source, that they should have the lead in interrogating her.

June 8, 1944

A few hours before the B17 landed in DC, a compromise was reached. The Office of Naval Intelligence would take the interrogation lead, but Johann Friedman would be part of the Interrogation and Evaluation Team, to provide interpretation, for as long as is necessary.

Director Kelly had Commander Price and Betty Lawrence meet the plane and take the passengers out to the Farm.

Anna was exhausted and in a daze. The presence of Betty helped reduce her anxiety, and she slept during the ride out to the farm.

The driver dropped Price and Johann off at the BOQ. Because there was no female quarters at the Farm, Betty took Anna to her cottage, which now contained a second bedroom.

Betty had no trouble understanding that Anna was pleased to use her tub, and spare nightgown. Later, Anna also enjoyed some toast and a pot of tea, fortified with brandy.

The next morning, their language barrier was still in place, but Betty helped Anna pick out a change of clothes from her wardrobe before taking her to the conference room at the Design Center, where they met Johann and Elmer for breakfast, and some initial discussions.

By the time they had finished breakfast Anna felt that these people were who she should relate the information Ernst wanted her to disclose.

During the rest of the morning, she told them who Ernst was, and tried to relate directly what he had related during their last night. She finished by giving Betty the film canister she had sewed into her bra.

They resumed after a break for lunch, while Betty had the film developed and printed. When they returned to the conference room, there were 24 prints on the wall. Elmer asked where they were taken.

Anna replied they were from inside the U 1701. One picture showed the sub from a dockside view. Elmer asked where that picture was taken.

"It's from the loading fueling dock underground sub

pens at the Deutche Werft AG shipyard in Hamburg.

Johann interrupted, "I just saw an intelligence report that there was a massive fire and explosion there recently. The fumes killed everything within a two mile radius of the shipyard. It had to be nerve gas."

Anna turned white, gasped, and said, "Ernst must have caused that. He said he would take care of it but I never thought...." And then she burst into tears.

Price concluded the meeting for the day and told Betty to bring Anna over to the big house for dinner, if she is up to it.

Johann and Betty took Anna back to Betty's cottage, and Anna retreated to her bedroom, refusing any dinner. She stated she just needed to be alone.

While Anna cried over her loss, Betty and Johann shared a sandwich and a stiff drink. They talked about Anna's near-term prospects, since she had no family in the states, and there was no way for her to safely return to Germany.

Johann said, "She's given us all the basic information, but may remember more. I think she, and I should stay here for a while. I'm sure Price will agree, and Donovan wants to keep me here as a spy on what you do here."

Betty had a sly look, and replied, "You are smitten with her, aren't you?"

"I can't lie, I'm looking forward to getting in her pants. I heard she showed her well developed tits to the English fishing boat, to get them to stop."

Betty poured them both another drink, and Johaan whispered, that during the flight, she told me a crewman on that boat tried to climb into her bunk with her."

"What did she do about it?"

She stuck an automatic pistol in his face and he took off running."

Betty observed, "You better not push her too soon, or too hard. She might blow a hole in you."

"Is that so?," He questioned.

Betty smiled and said, "I know a slightly older lady who is willing to occasionally keep you company until Anna is over her grief.

We'll need to be discrete, so she doesn't suspect we're more than friends. I do have an alarm clock that you can use to get back to the BOQ before she wakes up."

Johann rose at 5:00 AM, and returned to the BOQ.

The disclosures about the planned Rocket U-boat nerve gas attacks created a series of high level meetings to develop a counter to this new threat. The Project Javelin team in coordination with the OSS are charged with developing a response.

After OSS assets are unable to confirm where the Rocket U-boats will be built. Donovan suggests sending Anna back home to contact with her fiancee's Kriegsmarine Officer friends. She may find information leading to the location of the Rocket U-boats.

Johann is opposed to the idea, stating that it is too dangerous, but Anna demands the opportunity to return.

With pressure from both Donovan and Anna, the decision to have her return is finalized.

June 10, 1944

A team of manufacturing engineers from woodworking

companies around America are mobilized. They will work at the Raleigh site, developing the machines and processes to fabricate and assemble the airship designs coming out of the Fairfax Design Center.

June 12, 1944

A specially configured B-29 flew a high altitude reconnaissance mission over the Northwest end of Hokkaido. The photographs showed no activity, or any sign of life, in any of the four target areas.

The Iowa returned to service in July and is ready for duty in the South Pacific.

The war in the Pacific is far from over, but the noose around Japan is tightening. US submarines are sinking everything attempting to bring shipping to the Island Nation, and the Island Hopping Campaign is bringing Allied airfields ever closer to to the home islands.

The Propaganda Broadcasts created by Rio and Toshie, are causing widespread unrest, dissatisfaction, and mistrust of the Government and it's Military masters.

In the following months, the pace of the war increases, with the island hopping campaign in the South Pacific, the start of major supply convoys for Russia through the Suez Canal to the Black Sea, and support to resistance groups across Europe.

June 20, 1944

Johann and Anna ride the same English fishing boat into the North Sea, and Anna transfers to her father's boat. Johann will return to the contact location to receive her report in three weeks.

Anna starts visiting the club where she first met Ernst. On the third night she encounter's a junior officer who was a crewman on Ernst's sub. Shattered by his confirmation that Ernst was killed in the refueling accident, she allows the young man to comfort her.

He is enchanted by Anna, and the following night, she allows him to seduce her. Over the next two weeks, he reveals that the explosion and fire contaminated that section of the pen, and many workers were killed in an unsuccessful attempt to decontaminate that area. Eventually, the contaminated area was walled off, and the remaining pen is being rebuilt to convert and service the remaining Rocket U-boats. A new V4 loading and refueling area is constructed, and the next Rocket U-boat conversion is to be completed in August.

Work on the remaining U-boat conversions has already started and they are expected to be ready to depart for the US East Coast by October first. The last important fact she gleaned, was that the pen's 30 foot thick walls and roof had prevented any internal damage from either the 1941 large scale Lancaster bombing raids, or the recent B17 attacks.

July 10, 1944

Anna departs with her father at dawn, and the next day they meet Johann on the English fishing boat at sundown. Johann and her father exchange places for the evening after Anna refuses to return to England.

Anna spends the early evening giving a full briefing on everything she has learned, and gives him a written report she updated after every meeting with the young officer. Johann is shocked by the revelation of her seduction of him, but that action did obtain the necessary information in the shortest possible time.

She responded to his shocked look with the comment, "So I fucked him, to get him talking. It's not like I'm a virgin, or have anyone to be faithful to."

Johann flushed, stared at her a few seconds before saying, "I would like you to be faithful to me, if you'll agree to be my wife. I've been in love with you ever since we met."

Anna was not expecting that reaction. Her jaw dropped, and tears flowed for a moment, before her face hardened.

"I'm sure your offer is real, and I could easily fall in love with you. But, we both have other priorities now. I'm a good intelligence agent, and I can keep getting information, that you can't get any other way on the Rocket U-boat program. We have no choice, but to keep going until this war is over. There are only a few hours left before dawn. If you have no more questions, then make love to me before we need to part."

Included in the new information Johann sent to DC, was the fact that more attacks by B17s using conventional bombs would be unlikely stop completion of the Rocket U-boats. Even if B29s were available, It is doubtful that they could carry a big enough bomb to penetrate the pen roof.

A final element in the Rocket U-boat threat was the disclosure that they would be able to cross the Atlantic without surfacing using what they called a "snorkel". It was a pipe that could be extended above the surface to provide fresh air for the crew and the engines. The snorkel would be hard to spot visually, or with radar because it was only slightly larger than a periscope.

A.G. Kimbrough

Unrest across Europe is widespread, and a new Government in Britain is taking undercover steps to join the Allies in the expanding war against Germany and her Allies

Many senior German military leaders are aghast at Hitler's increasing madness, and another assassination plot develops under the code name Operation Valkyrie.

The plotters objectives are to eliminate Hitler, wrest control of the government from the Nazis, and seek a peace agreement with the Allies.

July 20, 1944

The plot to kill Hitler is culminated when Colonel Claus von Stauffenberg, chief of the army reserve, planted a bomb during a conference at "Wolf's Lair, a command post at Rastenburg, Prussia. Stauffenberg planted the explosive in a briefcase, which he placed under a table, then left quickly.

Hitler was studying a map of the Eastern front as Colonel Heinz Brandt, trying to get a better look at the map, moved the briefcase out of place, farther away from where the Fuhrer was standing. At 12:42 PM, the bomb went off. When the smoke cleared, Hitler was wounded, charred, and even suffered the temporary paralysis of one arm—but he was very much alive.

The subsequent investigation showed the extent of the conspiracy, and Hitler began the systematic liquidation of his enemies.

After The Days Of Infamy

More than 7,000 Germans would be arrested, and up to 5,000 would wind up dead—either executed or as suicides. Hitler, Himmler, and Goering took an even firmer grip on Germany and its war machine. Hitler was convinced that fate had spared him—"I regard this as a confirmation of the task imposed upon me by Providence"—and that "nothing is going to happen to me. The great cause which I serve will be brought through its present perils and everything can be brought to a good end.

August 1, 1944

Howard Hughes, Commanders Price, Wycliff, and Boyd are summoned to a meeting in Admiral Kings office. In addition to King, Army Generals Hap Arnold and Leslie Groves are present.

Mickey had reported plans for Mitsubishi to be building copies of the German Me 163 "Komet" rocket-powered interceptor. The plane, the Mitsubishi J8M (Shusui), would be built in large quantities with the highest priority, to meet the anticipated threat from the B29 heavy bombers.

The success of the Me 163 against the early B17 raids in Europe have the Army Air Force, and the Manhattan Project managers became very concerned.

The Javelin team were presented with a mission for the Lexington, sometime after March 30, 1945. The Lexington would be loaded exclusively with Mustangs. Their mission would be to use the Mustangs as fighter cover against the J8M interceptors, for a few special B-29 high altitude bombing mission. The Lexington must be ready to support this mission, even if it is necessary to slip the completion schedules on the follow-on airship carriers.

The was no discussion about the details of the bombing mission, and this mission is classified Top Secret Presidential.

August 5, 1944

Hitler orders the subs and V4s to be completed in time for a coordinated V4 nerve gas attack on North America by the fall of 1945. He also orders the V4 launch groups to be deployed against the Eighth Air Force bases currently sending B17 raids against German targets.

USS Lexington CVAS 1

Author Notes:

Thanks for reading this book. I will appreciate your positive review and any feedback or comments you may have. If you are interested in becoming a beta reader of my pre-release books, please contact me at:

agkatfri@mail.com

Other Books by A.G. Kimbrough

**https://www.amazon.com/A.G.-Kimbrough/e/
B008J28CME**

CPSIA information can be obtained
at www.ICGtesting.com
Printed in the USA
FSHW021941101218
54386FS